STEALING HIS HEART

NOX BAY PACK BOOK ONE

CONNOR CROWE

FATED FIRE FOUNDRY

When the kids are away, the mates will play…

Sign up here for your FREE copy of ONE KNOTTY NIGHT, a special story that's too hot for Amazon!

https://dl.bookfunnel.com/c1d8qcu6h8

Join my Facebook group Connor's Coven for live streams, giveaways, and sneak peeks. It's the most fun you can have without being arrested ;)

https://www.facebook.com/groups/connorscoven/

Vale Valley Valentines (multi-author series)

That Magical Moment

Nox Bay Pack

Stealing His Heart

Protecting His Heart

THE EYE OF THE OCEAN

One more mission. One last heist. Then I could leave this game for good. That was the deal.

I slunk through the shadows, grateful for the cloudy night. Moonlight lit up the grounds for only seconds at a time, leaving me ample opportunity to pass unnoticed. Proud pines stretched toward the sky and snow-tipped mountains crested the horizon. Each heavy bough of the passing trees sheltered my steps. They'd never see me coming.

Sneaking up on my prey was nothing new. Nor was infiltration, stealth, or secrecy. But tonight, a current of anxiety ruffled through my fur that I couldn't shake. Tonight, something was going to happen. Something, if my instincts were correct, that not even my training could prepare me for.

I kept my nose to the ground, searching for the scent of my target. It wasn't far now.

Normally I wouldn't have taken such a high-risk contract. But what can I say? Money talks. They'd set the price at a cool half a million for anyone who could retrieve the Eye of the Ocean, and it was just the break I needed to retire in style.

And if I, the fabled Crimson Fox, thief extraordinaire, couldn't retrieve it, then who could?

This should have been like any other mission. Just get in, get the artifact, get out. It wasn't like I was breaking into a prison or something. But this wasn't just any pack.

This was Nox Bay.

Few names inspired such fear in the shifter world. Rumors and speculation were rampant about the pack's violent nature, their brutal leadership, and most of all, their imposing Alpha. But as for real, eyewitness reports? No one had ever crossed them and lived to tell the tale.

That, combined with the exceeding rarity of the artifact, drove the price into the heavens. They said it had the power to control the element of water itself, one of four such artifacts called 'The Keys of Life.' I still wasn't sure about all of that, but what I was sure about was finishing the job and getting paid.

Tonight, I was going to pull off my biggest caper yet. Then I'd settle down with my winnings, find a nice, peaceful town by the sea, and leave the life of crime behind me.

Or so I thought.

It wasn't like I wanted to be a thief when I grew up. But as an omega fox shifter without a pack, I did what I had to do to survive--even if that toed the line of legality. A mysterious organization called The Black Hands took me in when I was no more than a pup, and there I learned everything. It wasn't easy, but it was a way of life. It was all I knew.

Footsteps shook me from my thoughts and I froze, pressing myself against a nearby tree. My ears pricked up and the steps grew closer.

Someone was here. Someone was watching. I held my breath and waited for them to pass. Seemed like ages passed. The steps slowed. Stopped. Then they moved on once more, around the corner and out of sight.

That was a close one. I peered around the corner to

make sure they were gone. From here, I had a straight shot to the door. Then I'd be in.

I took a deep breath, steeled myself, and leapt into the darkness, bounding quickly on my soft, furry paws toward the slowly closing door. Almost there, almost there...

I slipped through the cracks just as the door shuddered to a close. My tail whipped into the pack lands behind me, just a hair's breadth away from being caught in the closing gate. That was a close one, but I didn't have any time to celebrate. I was here for one thing, and one thing only.

The Eye of the Ocean.

I didn't know why everyone wanted to get their hands on it. I didn't much care either. I just knew that if I could lift it from the Nox Bay Pack and bring it back to my sponsor, I'd be half a million richer and no longer beholden to their schemes. I could finally live life the way I wanted, not the way someone had predestined for me.

My shifter senses pricked up on full alert as soon as I was in pack lands. I sniffed the air, searching for signs of nearby guards. The smell of wolf hung heavy in the air, yes, but it was a ways off yet. And what's more, I smelled the scent of ale mixed in with their earthy odors. Perhaps they were taking a little midnight booze break.

Worked for me.

I didn't waste any time. Keeping my head low and my back close to the buildings, I made my way across the enclave. I held the mental image of the crude map I'd seen in my mind, trying to remember where the most likely locations to find the Eye.

Around the corner. Through the tree-lined pathway (careful to keep away from the loose stones on the road). Past the tavern, where I could smell the scent of wolves and food from here. My stomach growled, but I paid it no mind. I was getting close. I could nearly taste it.

I didn't become the most sought after thief in the land by sitting around on my haunches. No, I worked for what I had, tooth and nail. That, and I had one ace in the hole that no one else knew about.

The frequencies of precious metals reverberated in my head like some kind of radar system. I could seek them out like no other, and my brain acted as some kind of walking metal detector. Didn't know why I could. Didn't matter. But in this line of work? It sure came in handy.

The pull of the Eye grew stronger and I ducked into an

alcove, holding my breath as a young child passed, holding her father's hand.

They'd just come out of a darkened building, long and flat with only a few windows. I stayed where I was and waited for them to pass out of earshot, hoping they hadn't noticed me. With the way the moon hid behind the pale wash of clouds tonight, I doubted it.

Ornate wooden engravings hung over the doorway, depicting scenes of battle from times long past. I almost stopped to look at them—the workmanship was fantastic—but I shook my head and pressed on. I was too close to my target to mess this up now.

This was almost too easy.

Where was the catch? Where was the alarm that would go off as soon as I crept near the artifact? And for that matter, where were the guards? None of this matched what I'd been told about Nox Bay. My fur bristled with a wave of anxiety. In this business, knowledge was power. And not knowing what was going on had the potential to get very, very bad.

I pushed the thoughts away and took in a cleansing breath. Worry about that later. Right now, the energy of the Eye was pulsing through my brain like a gong, drawing me ever closer.

Clenching my jaw, I slipped around the perimeter of the building, looking for an entrance. To go in through the front door wouldn't do—only a fool would try that. I'd nearly completed a full lap when I saw it, almost obscured by the low hanging fog of the night.

A small slatted window, probably left open for ventilation. It wasn't big enough for a man to fit through, or a wolf for that matter, but for a fox? I grinned.

It hovered two stories off the ground with not much surrounding it. A drain pipe led up the side of the building not far away, but I'd have to make a leap for it.

No problem for the Crimson Fox, I told myself, and dug my claws into the soft wood at the base of the building. I scaled quickly, my legs and arms working in tandem as the night air grew cool around my face. The ground dropped away below me and I clung to anything I could find—nails, eaves, shingles. My paws scraped against the drain pipe with an awful screech more than once and I froze, hoping against hope that no one would hear and investigate.

After what seemed like ages I was level with the opening, still a few feet to the left of me. I clung onto the boards anchoring me to the side of the building and stretched as far as I could. No luck.

I didn't want to get off balance and tumble to the hard-packed ground below. Didn't want to overextend myself. But it was close, so close, and I could almost reach it...

My claws latched onto the metal grating at the last second, just as my back paws slipped from the slippery pipe and I began to fall. The yanking motion of dangling from the rusty metal grate shot through my body. I winced and my feet scrabbled for purchase. I wasn't dead. Not yet.

I managed to hoist myself back up and onto the small ledge where the vent lay. My heart hammered quick in my chest, both from the excitement and the near-death experience. A pale blue-green light caught my eye through the grate and I stood transfixed. there it was. My prize.

The Eye of the Ocean was so much more beautiful than I'd heard about in the old stories. It glistened and fluctuated with light, drawing me in and holding me trapped, like a dragonfly in amber. It really was like looking into the sea, I realized with awe. No wonder men were so desperate to get their hands on it.

I stuck my snout through the opening first, stretching my body as thin as I could. One paw. Then the next. My fur caught on a sharp spike of metal. I winced, trying to wiggle free. This was what I was afraid of. The metal dug through my fur and into my skin, sending pain up my torso and setting off alarm bells in my head. If I got stuck here in this stupid grate...

I winced and flailed out with my paws, trying to find a grip on something. I braced, preparing for the pain, and pushed.

Spots danced before my eyes at the pain. The sound of ripping hair filled my ears as a tuft of fur came away. The momentum carried me the rest of the way and I tumbled into the building, my arms and legs windmilling through the air for a fraction of a second before I landed, hard. Dust flew up around me as wood splintered. Air rushed out of my lungs in a long whoop, leaving me breathless.

Well, if I hadn't gotten the wolves' attention before, I definitely had now.

"Getting sloppy, Fox." I could hear the growl of my sponsor now. I didn't want to think about what he'd do to punish me this time.

No. I squeezed my eyes shut and fought off the panic. That's why I was here. That's why I'd put myself through this trial, to get the Eye and get out of here. To get away from the Black Hands, and to finally build a life for me instead of someone else.

Now I just had to finish the job and get the hell out.

I forced myself to my feet, even though my chest was still seizing for air. It would come, I knew, but that didn't mean I wouldn't look like a drowning fish in the meantime. I swiped a paw across my blurry eyes and refocused. The glowing orb was still there, sitting on a pedestal not far from here. Its beauty threatened to hypnotize me all over again, but my paws itched and I bounded forward, desperate for a better look.

It sat on top of a marble pillar like some kind of trophy, filling the building with the light of the ocean. I'd 'retrieved' all manner of rare and valuable artifacts in my career, but nothing so stunning as this.

Something still ate at me, though. If this Eye of the Ocean was so valuable, then why weren't there guards? Why was I able to break into the building so easily? And why hadn't my fall triggered some kind of alarm?

I didn't like this. I didn't like this at all.

But what was I supposed to do, put my tail between my legs and head home? Not while I was this close.

The pedestal, and the orb, hung nearly four feet above

me. Not exactly fox-level. I'd have to shift back to human, and doing that would only expose me more.

That was the thing about shifting. Foxes didn't exactly wear clothes, and if I shifted now without my go-bag I'd stashed in the woods, I'd be...well...naked. And that was the last thing I needed.

I shifted my gaze up to the marble platform one more time, trying to see if there were any other routes I could take to get to the gem. Nothing came to me, and after my perilous fall into the building and through the grate (my side still ached something awful), I knew I only had one option.

I needed to shift.

So I rushed over into a dark corner, sucked in a breath, and tapped into that deep part of myself where my human counterpart rested. Immediately I felt him rushing to the surface, ready to stretch his legs and stand. I let the shift overtake me. No turning back.

Claws retracted and became fingernails. Fur faded away. My snout shortened into a small pink nose, and my ears returned to the sides of my skull as hair sprouted from my scalp once more. It wasn't a painful transformation, no--but it was intense. The rush of feelings and sensations both man and animal flooded over me and through me, and when I opened my eyes once more, I looked through human pupils.

Everything looked different from this vantage point. I was no longer nose to the ground and could see the layout of the building a lot better. My night vision had turned to crap, though, and I reached out a hand to steady myself on the nearby wall. The Eye of the Ocean peeked out at me, now directly at eye level. All I had to do was step forward and take it.

Too easy, my mind rebelled. Too easy.

This was worse than sneaking through the highest-security compounds where I could be discovered at any moment. At least then, I knew what I was up against. Here? I had no idea.

I squared my shoulders, fixed the image of the orb in my mind, and stepped toward it. So far, so good. One step. Two steps. Another. I stood right in front of the platform, so close now the moving colors flashed spots in my eyes. I stretched my fingers. Reached out.

And then I touched it.

Surprisingly warm to the touch, I cupped the Eye of the Ocean in my hands. My heart hammered out a frantic staccato that echoed in my ears. My breaths lodged in my chest. But nothing happened. No alarms went off.

No guards came rushing to attack me. No booby trap sprang and sent spikes raining down on me.

Nothing like that.

I'd simply waltzed in and taken the artifact. Something was seriously not right here.

I slipped the Eye into my bag and secured it against my waist. I headed for the door before my luck could run out but just as I reached the exit, I heard a strange, wailing sound that set my teeth on edge.

"Wait! No! Stop!"

I froze, listening. It was the first time I'd heard anyone else at all nearby, and they sounded like they were in trouble.

I pressed my ear to the wall and the sound of a scuffle reached me. More crying, kicking, running. And a crunching, bone-shattering fall.

Tired, terrified sobs.

"Please...don't..."

The scent of a fellow omega's heat caught my attention and I clicked together the pieces in my mind. Oh god. Someone was out there, an alpha most likely. And an omega, caught at the wrong place at the wrong time.

Another growl. Another cry.

I palmed the orb in my pocket as a war of values clashed in my mind. I could go. Hell, I probably should go. I could get the hell out while everyone else was distracted and I'd be home free with my prize.

But at what cost?

I was an omega, too. I knew how hard life had been for me, especially during my heats. I knew how some alphas didn't know how to take no for an answer, and how I'd had to learn to protect myself.

I couldn't leave him like that. It would haunt me forever, no matter how much money I made. I had to do something.

So I swallowed my fear, threw open the door and launched myself toward danger.

2

RED HANDED

"Get your hands off him."

I stood my ground as the leering alpha froze and turned to face me. He had a jagged cut down the side of his face and a sleazy, glassy look in his eye. Probably drunk. Beneath him was a whimpering, wriggling omega with a half-torn shirt and a bloody lip.

"Excuse me?" He rasped. The alpha's eyes raked up and down my naked body, widening when he saw that I, too, was an omega. "Get out of here or you'll meet the same fate."

This guy probably gargled nails for breakfast or something, but I couldn't just let him get away with it. I was naked, unarmed, and terrified—not to mention I was holding a very important stolen artifact.

I'd been in tough spots before, all part of the job. Just hoped I'd get out of this one alive. My eyes flicked around the periphery, looking for a weapon, a distraction, anything. I could shift back to fox form and attack, but I feared for the safety of the Eye if I did so. My hand brushed an old dusty jug on top of one of the storage crates. Perfect.

My fingers clasped around it and I launched forward, raising it over my head with all my might.

"Hey alphahole, I said get off him!"

He turned just in time to get a face full of glass. His nose crunched and blood spewed, splattering to the ground in the moonlight. The omega screamed and covered his face, using the momentary distraction to gain his feet. He looked at me with wide, terrified eyes, and I didn't waste any time.

"Go!" I shouted at him. "Now!"

He opened his mouth like he wanted to say something, but the alpha blinked and shook his head, no longer dazed by the blow. He turned tail and ran, disappearing off into the woods.

And now that left me. Still naked. Still a thief. And still tangled up with a very violent alpha.

Shit.

The alpha looked even more haggard now with a bloody nose and a piece of glass still sticking out of his cheek. He didn't seem to care, though, as he advanced on me with that same predator's grin.

"Guess you'll just have to do instead, pretty boy," he growled. "I told you not to mess with what's mine. What the fuck are you, anyway? Too small, too puny for a wolf."

He swiped out a fist at me but I ducked and rolled away just in time, leaving him sprawling from the momentum. All the while, I clasped the bag holding the Eye to me as close as I could, praying it wouldn't spill and reveal my secret...

"Come back here!" The alpha roared. I didn't stop to look over my shoulder. I turned and made a run for it, my eyes set on the grove of trees marking the edge of pack lands. If I could just get there and lose myself in the forest...maybe shift and hide out till they were gone...

Too late.

The alpha pummeled into me and breath heaved out of my lungs as I fell to the ground. My face hit the dirt. My head spun. A vicious wolf shifter hovered over me, practically slobbering at my pain. I was sure it was the end for me, but then my bag flew away from my side and spilled open.

I watched in stunned horror, opening my mouth to scream but unable to find the air. The Eye of the Ocean rolled out of the bag, rolled across the dusty ground, until it came to a stop. Right beneath a studded leather boot.

I held my breath and traced my gaze upward. The alpha on top of me flew to attention, scrambling back to his feet immediately.

"What's the meaning of this?" The newcomer asked, scowling first at my attacker, then at the Eye, then at me.

"We've got a thief on our hands, Cade." the alpha sneered. "I was just doing my civic duty to apprehend him."

Cade, dressed in some sort of guard's uniform, wasn't impressed. "Watch it, Galt." He spat each word like poison. "I can't keep covering for you, and if you hadn't been...occupied," he snarled, "maybe this wouldn't have happened in the first place."

That seemed to get through to him at last. His face blanched. He lowered his head in submission, exposing his neck. I should have used the momentary distraction to get up and run, but if I did that now, the Eye and everything I'd worked for would be lost.

Cade crouched down and picked up the Eye, staring for a moment into its luminous depths. "How the hell did he get in?" He growled at Galt. "You were supposed to be on watch."

Galt visibly gulped. He opened his mouth to speak but Cade cut him off with a wave of his hand.

"You know what? Forget it. We're taking him to Markus. Come on."

Markus. Something about that name rang a bell deep inside me, like I'd heard it before but couldn't remember where.

I yelped as Cade grabbed me by the arm and wrenched me up, forcing me to stand. My body cried out in pain from the chase and the attack, but I was too weak to shift now. Too weak to run.

Guess the Crimson Fox had finally been caught red-handed.

THE UNEXPECTED THIEF

"Alpha Markus."

"What is it?" I roused from my near-slumber, looking up to see the messenger in my doorway. Couldn't a guy get some shut-eye? Not when you were the pack alpha of Nox Bay, apparently.

"There was an intruder on our lands. He tried to steal the Eye."

That woke me up in an instant. I shot to my feet and watched the messenger with a wary glance. My heart tumbled over itself. Our most precious relic...without it our pack would be nothing. "Well?" I asked, not waiting for a response. "Did you catch him?"

"We did, sir. Awaiting your judgement as we speak."

I scrubbed a hand over my face and yawned. "I'll be right there. See to it that he's properly detained."

"Of course, sir."

He left the room and I stood alone, watching my reflection in the mirror. It had been so long since we'd had any intruders on our land. Of course, we had a reputation to maintain as the biggest and most notorious pack out there. Those who stumbled across us never left for a reason, and I needed to make sure I impressed that same fear on our would-be thief.

I took a breath, smoothed my hair, and got dressed. An alpha's work was never done.

———

"Come forward," I called to the guards at the door. I'd taken up residence in the rough-hewn wooden "throne" in the pack hall and ordered the prisoner brought to me. It was all part of the theatrics, of course, but I couldn't have anyone leaving the pack thinking that we were soft.

The iron-banded doors banged open and two guards stomped in, nearly dragging a smaller man between them.

Two things caught my eye immediately.

One: he was an omega.

And two: he was naked.

But when the sad, battered omega lifted his head and met my eye with such a fierce, defiant gaze, that's when I lost it completely.

This was no mere petty thief. When our eyes locked I saw within him, all the way down to the depths of his soul. I saw his past, his anger, his heartbreak. It was this ability to read people, after all, that had gained me Pack Alpha status in the first place.

And when I looked upon this omega, I knew without a doubt in my heart that he was my fated mate.

Suddenly, "it's complicated" didn't even begin to cover it.

Only problem was, I had a job to do. A duty to my pack and my family. Nox Bay didn't get to be the most feared and revered pack by going easy on intruders, but this...this was my mate. I knew it, sure as I knew the sun set in the evening.

I couldn't exactly say that in front of a room full of my most trusted advisors and clansmen, though.

So I put on my most intimidating face, drew myself up to my full height, and approached.

My heart thudded in time with my steps as I drew near to the omega. His scent wove around me and through me, muddying my senses. In all my years as Pack Alpha, I'd never met someone so entrancing, and now here he was, a sworn enemy.

His tanned skin was lean and muscular with more than a few scrapes and scars. I wanted to trace them with my fingers, learn each of their stories. But that would have to be for another day.

I waved the guards away from him and they released his arms. The omega swayed slightly, but held his ground. His eyes, though—those maddening, gold-flecked eyes— never left mine.

"Tell me your name." Not only because it was part of protocol, but because I wanted to feel each syllable on my tongue.

The omega coughed and winced, pressing a hand to his side. A long, bleeding scratch caught my eye and instantly my wolf cried out. I wanted to help him, to dress his wounds and make sure he never hurt again.

Where was all this coming from?

I shook my head, cleared my thoughts, and continued on.

"Tell me your name, boy."

He finally broke eye contact and stared at the ground, a sigh escaping his full, pink lips. "Felix."

Whether that was his real name or not, I didn't know.

"And tell me Felix, what were you doing on my pack lands?"

He didn't answer. The guards stepped toward him but I waved them off. No. I would talk to this one alone.

"You tried to take something," I continued, pacing around him in a wide arc. "Something that belongs to me." I could see that his hands were bound from behind with special cuffs. Kept them from shifting.

But he didn't look like a wolf. What *was* he?

Still Felix didn't answer. I didn't blame him. Anything he said would likely only get him in deeper trouble at this point, and thieves like him were always trained not to talk.

"You know we don't take kindly to intruders on our land here in Nox Bay. Surely you've heard the stories." I rounded on him just in time to give him my most menacing glare.

Don't think about him naked. He's a criminal. A thief. He needs to be treated as such.

I forced out a breath through my nose and prepared to deliver the sentence. As much as it pained me, I had to do it. I could figure out this whole 'fated mate' business later.

"The rules are clear on stealing. We don't tolerate it. Period. Usually we'd cut off a hand or two to teach you a lesson."

Felix froze. I could feel the anxiety and fear coming off of him in waves, but kudos to him—he didn't show it outwardly.

"But," I said, measuring my words carefully, "I'm feeling unnaturally merciful today. I'm going to give you a choice, Felix."

Because prisoners who thought they had a choice in their own demise were always more pliable, I remembered.

"You can stay here in Nox Bay as our prisoner and work off your crime, or I'll have one of my men here cut off a hand and send you on your way. Pack life here is different than you're probably used to, and I won't promise an easy life, but if you do good work and are respectful of me and my pack, we won't have any problems."

By now the guards on either side of me were ogling at my show of trust in the young omega. They were right to be—usually we'd just punish the poor sap and move on, but something about this particular omega pulled at my heartstrings in a way no other man had.

"What'll it be?" I asked him. I knew which one I secretly hoped he would pick, but...

Felix's eyes met mine once more and within them I saw a myriad of emotions flash through in an instant. Fear, guilt, anger, defiance, those were all there—but there was something else trapped just beneath the surface. Something that called out to me. That called out to be claimed.

"You're..." Felix spoke at last. "You're not going to kill me?" His voice was ragged and dry, each word coming out like a cough. "Thought that's what you guys did."

Cade flicked a wary glance at me, his hand still on the butt of his weapon.

I towered over him, letting my alpha pheromones out to play just enough to mollify him, make him receptive to what I said next.

"Make your choice, omega." The words came out as a growl that vibrated from my chest all the way down to my toes.

"I...don't want to lose a hand. Please. I never meant to be a thief in the first place, I..."

"Save it," I snapped.

The guards stepped forward, looking a little too pleased about manhandling the weakened omega. Pack or not, their shiny-eyed glances made me a little queasy.

"You're dismissed." I didn't take my eyes off Felix, still kneeling naked and watching me with something between terror and awe.

First: he needed some clothes, or my wolf was going to go bonkers. And second: I needed to get him into his room and the hell away from me.

"Alpha Markus?" Cade asked, his eyes flicking to the prisoner.

"I said dismissed."

They turned and left the hall, filing away with the rest of my team. Soon only the young omega and I were left in the throne room. I could hear his breathing quicken, hear the race of his heart thudding off the stone walls. I watched him for a moment, only a moment, and offered him my hand.

"Come along," I commanded. "I'll take you to your room now."

His eyes widened at that, his mouth opening in a little circle of surprise. "You said I'm your prisoner."

"You are. Now come on or I'll have my men drag you."

He gulped, his pretty little throat working, and I helped him to his feet, leading him out of the throne room and into his new life.

Goddess help me.

4

GOLDEN HANDCUFFS

My heart thudded in time with my steps across the hard stone floor. My feet felt every ridge, every crack of the tiles. My bare skin prickled with a combination of goosebumps and sweat.

In all my years of work, I'd never been caught like this before. I'd been careless. I'd been stupid. And I knew that no help would come.

If anything happens in the field, they'd always told us, it was on us to get out of it. Couldn't have a secret criminal syndicate blowing their cover by extracting an agent who'd fucked up, right?

I sighed and squeezed my eyes shut for a moment. I focused on putting one foot in front of the other.

I should never have come here—but then again, it wasn't like I'd had much of a choice.

We passed a series of long hallways and sturdy buildings. I craned my neck upward, trying to discern direction by the stars. Couldn't. Too cloudy. I did, however, catalog possible exits and the places I saw guards. I'd need to know where I was going when I escaped.

And oh, I planned to. No one kept the Crimson Fox tied up for long.

I bit my lip and strained against the cuffs on my wrists. If I could just shift, I could flee. But try as I might, I couldn't contact that part of myself. Like someone had thrown up a barrier deep within me, keeping me chained to this form.

Bastards.

"You will wake at seven o' clock every morning. You will return to your room by ten o' clock each night. You will have meals with us in the main hall, and you will report to me directly for your duties of the day. Are we understood?"

"Yeah," I grumbled, though I wasn't excited about having to see the infuriating alpha for work every day. From the moment I laid eyes on him, something had shifted within me. It was more than just the terror of being caught—this was something bigger. Deeper. And it scared the hell out of me.

When those asshole guards brought me before Alpha Markus, I'd known I was a dead man. No one crossed Nox Bay and lived. Why else had we never heard or seen anyone come back?

But then things had changed. Instead of killing me, they wanted to keep me...and that didn't make sense at all.

Rookie mistake, I thought to myself as we approached a locked door. A guard stood outside and gave the alpha a nod as we passed through.

"Here we are," Markus said, stepping back to let me view the room.

I don't know what I'd been expecting. Well, actually, I did. Some kind of dank cell with bars on the windows and a cold, wet stone floor. Basically, a dungeon.

But this room wasn't that at all. It was actually quite nice. Nicer than the shabby dorms at the Black Hand compound, that was for sure.

A soft carpet covered the floor in tones of mossy green and a rough-hewn wooden bed sat in front of a wide window overlooking the courtyard. A large crimson tapestry hung on the wall, wool by the look of it. What was especially odd, however, was how my sharpened senses pinged at something just beyond it.

Something metal.

I kept the shock from my face and put on a neutral expression to turn to the alpha. He was yammering on about something else that I hadn't quite picked up on, and I only hoped it wasn't important.

"..and that's about all there is to it," he finished, crossing his arms. "Any questions?"

I blinked and looked around the room. Nothing special, no, but way more than I deserved as a prisoner. Just what was their game here?

The question crystallized on my tongue when I faced the alpha once more. Something about him flowed over me like warm honey, making it hard to think. A strange sense of ease filtered through my veins. Made me feel safe. Safer than I ever had with the Black Hands. But that was nonsense, right? Total nonsense.

This pack couldn't be trusted, everyone knew that. And if I let my guard down, I'd pay for it. No. The only thing to focus on right now was waiting for the alpha to leave and hatching a plan to get the hell out of here.

These stupid anti-shifter cuffs posed a bit of a problem, though...

"You gonna make me wear these the whole time?" I asked, waving my arms from behind my back. "My shoulders are killing me already."

"We can't take any chances." Markus avoided my gaze. What if he was thinking the same thing I was?

"I'm not gonna shift and run off," I lied. "Where would I even go anyway? You've got wolves everywhere, and I'd have to get out of this room first."

Please let me go, I prayed under my breath. *Please let me go, please let me go.*

Markus considered for a moment, then stepped forward until his face was only inches from mine. I froze. He was close enough now that I could feel the embrace of his body heat and the strong, spicy scent of his wolf. It curled into me like a wayward puff of smoke, slow at first, and then more, and more...

Fire. Pine. Honey. For a terrible moment, I lost all sense of reason and tilted my head to the side out of instinct, wanting to be closer to him. Wanting him to claim me.

Markus sucked in a breath and time spun out before us

as the connection grew stronger. I wanted him. By all the gods, I wanted him.

I was so fucking screwed, and not in the fun way.

The spell broke not a second too soon, though. For both of us. "Behave," he rumbled, his voice so deep it vibrated all the way to my heart. "Don't make me regret this."

Then he wrapped his arms around me, almost like a hug. I sucked in a quick little gasp, as his hands brushed mine. He was so warm, so close, so intoxicating...

Click. The cuffs came free and Markus drew away, the same awe and longing dancing in his eyes. He looked away.

"There." He said, his back to me now. "But if I hear so much as the smallest transgression...my mercy has its limits." Markus looked over his shoulder, and any hint of the desire I'd once seen on his face was gone. This was all cold, hard alpha power.

I gulped. "Thank you." And I felt it, too. I'd thought for sure I'd be dead right about now. I still didn't understand the source of the alpha's sudden mercy, but I wasn't going to question it. As long as I was still alive, I could escape. I could still finish the mission, and I could still get paid.

"I'll let you rest, for now. There is a small selection of clothing in the trunk by your bed. Do let the guard know if you need another size. But Felix? Don't even think about leaving. We are watching twenty four seven. If you try anything...we'll know."

With that final, menacing message, the door closed and locked me in.

All the energy left my limbs the moment the door clicked into place. Now that I was alone, I had no one to impress. No false persona to put on. The truth was, I was tired.

Bone tired.

I sunk into the bed, moaning in relief as the fluffy blankets wrapped around me. All of the adrenaline had eked out of my system at last, and I could barely move I was so drained.

A nagging current of dread still swirled in my gut when I thought about my sponsor back at the compound. What would happen when I didn't return? Would they come looking for me? Would they even care?

And then came the most unsettling thought of all: did I want to go back to that life, even if I could?

5

MISPLACED FAITH

What the hell had I gotten myself into?

I scrubbed a hand over my face and forced myself to walk away from the door. Silence stretched out around me, sucking all the oxygen from the air. This was wrong. This was so, so wrong.

Not gonna lie to you. It was hard walking away from my mate like that. Really hard.

But how could we ever be together? I was the Pack Alpha of Nox Bay, sworn to protect this land and my family. And he was an intruder and a thief. Not to mention his shifter form wasn't even a wolf.

I could tell that much as soon as I set eyes on him. He

carried himself differently. Smelled differently. But if he was no wolf, then what was he?

I sighed and pinched the bridge of my nose. My duty, first and foremost, was to my pack. And some day soon, I'd need to mate and produce an heir. It was the fate ordained to me since birth. People expected things of me. And I wouldn't let this omega, no matter how entrancing, tear that apart.

"There you are."

The words startled me more than they should have. I snapped to attention to find my second there, regarding me with curiosity.

"Arric," I greeted him, but kept walking.

"Red." He used the familiar version of my last name, the one he only used when he needed my full attention.

"It's late." I checked my watch. "Or rather, early. What is it?"

Arric fell into step beside me, his long legs easily keeping up with mine. "If I may speak freely."

"You may."

"The thief. Why did you let him live?"

I considered that for a moment. Why indeed? It would

40

have been so easy to just send him away, have him executed or maimed. We had to set an example, after all. An attempt to steal our most precious artifact could not go unpunished.

Then, of course, was the call in my heart the moment I laid eyes on him. The sad, troubled history behind those defiant eyes. The protective urge that swelled up inside me and wanted more than anything to protect him from the horrors of the world.

I couldn't say that, though.

"We could use an extra pair of hands around here." I suggested, keeping my voice casual.

Arric shook his head. "That's a weak excuse, Red. What happened?"

Why wouldn't he just leave me alone? I quickened my steps, but I knew Arric wouldn't leave until he got the truth. Or at least, as close to the truth as I was gonna give him.

"Have you secured the Eye?" I asked, trying to change the subject. "That's what we should be focusing on. Why was it left unguarded in the first place?"

Arric's face hardened, his lip curling upward. The depths of a snarl began to rise up from his chest. "That's the other thing I wanted to talk to you about. I had one of those dreams again."

I didn't have to ask to know what he meant. Prophetic dreams. One of the many talents our little pack had to offer. "And you saw the Eye in danger?"

"More than that," he said. His shoulders sagged like he was carrying a great weight. "Come here, I'll show you."

He turned a corner and we stepped into a small alcove. A cool wind howled through the walkway and scattered dead leaves across the ground. Arric glanced around for a moment before glancing at me. "Do you trust me, Red?"

"You know I do," I said, "But what does this have to do with—"

"Look."

He put his hands on my shoulders and the world turned white. Then there they were. I saw the building where we kept the Eye. I saw Galt, the night guard, stalking through the shadows. He lifted his nose to the sky and flicked his gaze around, picking up on a scent. Then I watched in horror as he left his post, gaining on the poor omega, pinning him, ignoring his cries for help...

I came back to myself shaking and covered in sweat,

bracing myself against the cold stone pillar. "Galt," I breathed, my jaw clenching. I could barely speak, the rage flared so high within me. I was ready to shift right then and there. There was one thing I couldn't abide, and as the Pack Alpha I had a duty to keep my brothers and sisters safe.

And to think, I'd actually placed that snake in a position of power...

I tasted iron and spat, realizing that I'd been biting the inside of my cheek. "Did he think he wasn't gonna get caught?"

Arric shrugged. "Alphas like that don't much care for rules, I've noticed. He probably would have gotten away with it too if it weren't for your little thief. Felix, I think his name was?"

Just the sound of his name sent me into protector mode. Damn him.

"What about him?" I asked, keeping my jaw clenched. My blood still ran high with the revelation about Galt but now fear and disgust ran through my veins as well.

"He interrupted their little, um, rendezvous. That's how they caught him in the first place."

Little by little, the pieces clicked together.

That's why he'd been caught. That's why Cade and Galt had dragged him here in the first place. He'd been at the wrong place at the wrong time...

Or the right place.

The sickening feeling only grew when I realized how close Felix had come to getting hurt. I shouldn't have worried about him, I knew that, but my gut twisted at the thought. With Galt occupied, he could have escaped. Could have taken the Eye and ran.

But he didn't.

He stayed, and he saved that omega from Galt's attack.

I knew there had been something special about him, but now I was realizing I didn't even know the half of it.

It took everything in me to keep from running off to check on him. What if Galt found him and wanted revenge? What if he tried to escape?

"Go round up Galt and Cade," I ordered Arric. "Throw them in the cells and let them think about what they've done."

"What happened to 'it's late'?" He gave me a tired smile, but still stood as obedient and ready as ever.

"Fuck what time it is. I need those bastards dealt with

now!" I nearly roared the words and my fingernails sharpened into claws as the wolf took hold. I couldn't let anything happen to him.

My omega. My mate. He'd risked his life and his prize to save another, someone who didn't mean anything to him.

It was up to me to repay that kindness.

"Now," I growled again when Arric hadn't moved.

"Sir!" Arric yelped and ran off, leaving me agitated and alone.

I took in shaky, labored breaths and tried to stop shaking. I couldn't. First to find out my guards were preying on pack omegas, and then to find that our new guest had nearly met the same fate...

I saw red. Fuck the rules. I needed to make sure he was safe.

Before I quite knew where my legs were heading, I was making a path back to Felix's room, praying that nothing had happened. Not yet.

———

Why is it that whenever you're heading somewhere in a

hurry, everyone and everything tries to hold you up? Distraction after distraction presented itself, and it was hours before I finally made it back to Felix's room.

"Have you seen him?" I panted at the confused guard. "He still in there?"

The guard, Adam if I remembered correctly, raised a concerned eyebrow. "You only left a few hours ago. Haven't seen anyone coming or going since then."

"But are you sure?" I asked, my voice rising. I knew, *knew* that I was being irrational, but in the heat of the moment I was powerless to stop it. "I just had a bad feeling and..."

"By all means, you can check again yourself if you like. I'm sure he's still in there, safe and sound just like you left him." Adam looked dubious, but unlocked the door.

I rushed into the room, knowing that I'd find him there, knowing that he'd look at me with those defiant eyes and ask why I was back so soon.

I was overreacting. Totally overreacting.

At least, I thought I was.

But when I rushed into the room, the omega was nowhere to be found.

6

BAD LUCK

I didn't feel great about it, but what choice did I have?

I sure wasn't going to let them keep me here, no matter how nice it seemed. Was probably a trick. Something to keep me docile until they could have their way with me. What reason did I have to trust them, anyway?

The bed, comfortable as it was, felt almost too real. Too good to be true. I was a prisoner, I reminded myself. And no matter how much they tried to butter me up, it wouldn't change that fact.

When I couldn't stand the stillness any longer, I got up and paced around the room. The Eye was still out there, calling to me with a faint, but traceable signal. If I could

47

make another attempt and actually retrieve it this time, maybe I could save the mission after all. Maybe I wouldn't be in for the beating of my life once (if ever) I returned to the compound.

I caught sight of my face in the mirror and frowned, realizing for the first time how thin I'd become. Months of hard work, little pay, and even less food had taken their toll on me, and it was starting to show. How long could I keep this up? How many more times could I risk my life before it all shattered around me?

I closed my eyes and drew in a breath, just like my mentor had taught me. I worked to find clarity, to ease the buzzing of thoughts and fears and pain. But as anyone who's tried to meditate knows, peace so rarely comes to those actively seeking it.

Every time my breaths began to slow into a rhythm, the alpha's face appeared in my mind's eye. And not only that. His face. His body. His clothes. His scent.

It wasn't even near time for my heat, so it couldn't be that, but something about this alpha set me off in new and terrifying ways. All the more reason I had to get out of here, artifact or not.

The metallic signal from behind the tapestry called out

to me again the closer I got to it. Lovely as it was, there was nothing metal about it, unless...

I picked up the thick wool and peeled it upward. There, beneath several layers of paint, was the outline of a door. Time and age had hidden it well enough, but not from me. Hope sprang anew—could this be my way out?

About chest height and just big enough for a small person to fit through, it had be some kind of tunnel. Perhaps a dumbwaiter. Or maybe it was just a long forgotten utility panel. That would suck.

I held my breath and clawed at the paint, trying to find purchase. Paint flecked away and fluttered to the ground. Once I had it started, I peeled away layer after layer until the door remained. Old, rusty—but still a door. And still my only way out of here.

Paint and grime dug under my nails and scratched at my skin, but I didn't care. Didn't even care that I was still naked. This was my chance, and I didn't think I was gonna get another one. I hooked my fingers into an indentation in the metal, gritted my teeth, and pulled.

A long, whining metallic sound screeched through the room as the door came free, opening onto into darkness. I winced and froze, hoping the guard hadn't heard anything. I didn't know how well these walls were insulated, but I didn't want to take any more chances than I had to. I peered into the hole and felt around with my hands. Nothing but dead air.

I couldn't tell how far down it went or if it even went anywhere at all. Maybe it had just been used for storage way back when. My heart pattered fiercely, my fox ready to pounce and get the hell out of here. Sweat stuck to my brow.

I leaned further in, as far as I could go without losing my balance, and then I felt the cool metal on the opposite wall. It was about three feet deep, then. My fingers closed over a metal bar bolted to the wall. I felt along its smooth edges—a rung.

A ladder.

"Looks like the Crimson Fox hasn't been caught yet," I muttered under my breath. I yanked at the rung, making sure it was stable. Then I slung myself inside and out of sight.

———

I descended for what felt like forever. Each little creak, each slip of my bare feet on the ancient rungs shocked through me like lightning. If I was caught again, there would be no mercy. Of that much I was sure. Total darkness surrounded me. My only anchor was the warm puff of each breath, and the feeling of the metal beneath my hands and feet.

How embarrassing would it be to nearly escape, only to fall and break my neck at the last second?

I nearly lost my balance when I finally reached solid ground once more. A small tunnel stretched out in front of me and through it I could see a small slant of light. The air hung heavy with dirt and dust. How long had it been since anyone had been down here? And what was this tunnel for in the first place?

My fox ached to shift and run free. Naked and human, I was weak. Vulnerable. Easy to catch, easy to kill. But as a fox, I could flee the scene and disappear into the woods without leaving a trace.

I wanted to shift. I needed to. But no matter how deeply I reached within, how much my fox cried out to reunite us once more, I just...couldn't.

I squeezed my eyes shut. Winced. Grunted.

Nothing.

"Motherfucker," I cursed under my breath. I wasn't even wearing the cuffs anymore. What had they done to me?

Fear lashed out now, wrapping around my heart. What if I could never shift again? What if they'd severed the connection somehow?

I swallowed against the lump in my throat. Perhaps this had been their plan all along. Who needed violence when there were much more subtle, much more agonizing ways to kill a man?

My shifter side had saved my ass more times than I could think. It kept me safe. Kept me warm on the cold streets before the Black Hands took me in. Helped me find work. Helped me get paid.

If I didn't have that anymore...what was I?

My hands balled into fists, chest heaving. I could worry about that later, when I was out of harm's way. Didn't make the emotion any less raw, any less terrifying, but it would have to do.

I followed the tunnel with a hand to the wall, passing over twists, turns, and dead ends. The air grew less stale as I ascended, switch back after switch back leading me toward the surface. Finally, with a cool breeze and a gasping breath of life, I found the exit.

A small trapdoor, probably just as overgrown with moss and weeds as the original room had been with paint, rested just above my head. I could still see prickles of sunlight creeping through the cracks and hear the chittering sounds of wildlife above me.

Once I got above ground, there would be no hiding any longer. I'd have to get my bearings and get the hell out, fast. There was no telling where I'd surfaced, and even my talented sense of navigation had been muddled by so many turns in the dark.

Once I opened this door, there would be no turning back.

I tried once again to shift, to contact the fox dwelling in my soul. No matter what I tried, however, it remained just out of my reach.

If I ever ran into those wolf bastards again, I vowed, I'd make them pay. I'd make them undo what they'd done to me, and make sure it never happened again.

For now, though? It was fight or flight. That simple.

I took a deep breath and pushed upward, letting the dirt and dust from the forgotten door rain down on my head.

———

Sunlight.

Bright and blinding.

I squinted my eyes against the sudden intrusion and peered out across the landscape.

Trees, roots, and stumps surrounded me. Rocks scattered across a long-forgotten path. No one was in sight. No one, at least, that I could see.

I turned, trying to get my bearings. Just because I wasn't surfacing into an ambush didn't mean I was home free. By the location of the sun I appeared to be facing west, and that meant...

A tall, barbed wire fence stretched tall and ominous behind me.

I blinked, heart racing faster.

I was out.

I was free.

That fence marked the edge of Nox Bay territory, and whoever had built this tunnel had led me right to the pack borders.

I should have been excited. Overjoyed, actually. I'd escaped Nox Bay and lived to tell the tale. There was still the matter of not being able to shift, and I'd attract attention running around as a naked human, but for now, I was free.

They wouldn't come beyond their lands looking for me —they were much too secretive for that.

But as I stood there, staring at the fence and reveling in my newfound freedom, I realized something even more disheartening.

I couldn't go home.

Life in the Black Hands had never been easy. In fact, it was downright brutal at times. If they hadn't brought me in off the streets when I was a kid then I probably wouldn't be alive today. But at what cost?

The alpha wolf's features flashed through my memory once more, startling up a new and confusing combination of feelings.

The Black Hands were using me and the other omegas to achieve their greedy ends. I knew that. But at the same time, it was all I had. All they made us believe we would ever be good for. I may have been a celebrated thief, but in reality? I was no more than their slave.

There was another problem, too—I still didn't have the Eye. The thought of going back to the compound empty-handed—not an option.

So there was really only one thing to do. I needed to flee.

Looked like I'd gotten my wish to get out and start a new life after all.

———

This sure would be easier in fox form.

My body ached and my soft human skin scratched against the twigs and fallen leaves. I moved as quietly as I could, but it still felt like a cacophony when I was used to moving in fur.

Damn wolves. Damn them all.

I continued to move west, staying beneath the shade and thick clusters of trees. I didn't see another man for hours, and for a moment I wondered if I'd surfaced into some parallel world.

My mind had plenty of time to stew on things as I crept toward safety. I was completely and totally alone now. No one to look out for me. No one to stand up for me if I got lost or hurt.

In a way, it was exhilarating. Not that I thought I could ever fully escape the Black Hands' mighty reach, but if I could just get far enough away...

Stupid idea. I know. But I was naked, cold, and hurting. The compound would never take me back after botching such an important mission, and if they did? I had no stomach for the "discipline" my mentor would dole out this time.

So I was lost. Alone. And since I couldn't access my fox, I was pretty much dead meat.

As if agreeing with me, a single, ear-splitting howl cut through the air. Then another.

The sound chilled me to my bones.

Wolves.

My feet were moving before my brain could fully process the information. Wolves were nocturnal, weren't they? They shouldn't be out, not right now...

Nox Bay. What if they were back? What if they were tracking me?

I ran, unmindful of where I was heading. *Flee*, my omega senses reared up within me. *Flee!*

So much for being a badass thief. So much for being the Crimson Fox. Sheer terror had taken over my body, and my only goal was self preservation.

Flee, my mind cried. *Flee, while you still can!*

The word bounced in my brain like a drum until I heard their footfalls behind me.

I didn't look back. I couldn't. Their long fangs, drooling maws, fierce muscles would be on me in an instant—if I didn't trip and break a leg first.

I ran, my legs burning and chest heaving. I ran, until the trees fell away and the ground turned rocky. I ran, until the ground ran out.

My feet skidded on the gravel and stopped just in time. A sheer drop spread out below me, plunging twenty feet or more into a creek. The ground was soft here, already crumbling under the weight of my approach. My hands grasped out for something, anything to hold on to. Nothing came.

The ground shifted and gravel clattered off the edge, splashing into the shallow water below. One look down at the craggy stone littered bank, and I knew I wouldn't make it.

And for my other option? Becoming the snack of two hungry wolves.

Just my fucking luck.

I reeled and windmilled my arms, trying to keep from tumbling over the edge. I couldn't shift. I couldn't jump. I couldn't fight them.

Couldn't fight them and win, anyway.

Another howl rang out, right behind me. My blood turned to ice, but an eerie sense of calm passed over me. This was it. If I was going to go, I'd go out fighting.

I balled my fists. If I was going to meet Death today, I would meet her head on.

7

SACRIFICE

 new howl cut through the air.

This one was different.

This one was almost...familiar.

Maybe I was hearing things. Maybe my brain was going haywire in the last moments of my life. But I could have sworn that howl *spoke* to me.

Take heart, it whispered. *You are safe now.*

Steeled by that final call, I opened my eyes to face my attackers.

A huge grey wolf launched out from the tree line, fangs bared, claws out. Easily twice the size of the other wolves, he barreled into them without mercy. They yelped and snapped at him, claws and fur flying in a frenzy too fast for my eyes to follow.

The huge wolf had come out of nowhere. I hadn't heard his steps approach like the others. I watched, frozen and curling into myself at the edge of the cliff as they fought for dominance. The larger wolf growled so deep I felt it in my belly. His fangs sunk into the other wolf's flesh and blood flew, spattering the pale, rocky ground.

In another instant both wolves were on him, growling and scratching and biting. Despite his size, fighting off two adult wolves was no easy task, even for this giant.

Time seemed to pass in slow motion as I watched them fight. For a brief second, the newcomer's huge golden eyes met mine.

Oh my god.

It was *him*.

I leapt out of the way of the snarling mess just in time. My back scraped against loose stones and I hissed in pain, but it didn't have time to register. Something else had taken up residence there and outweighed everything else.

My fox surged to the surface, glowing hotter and brighter like a new ember.

Where before there was only silence, now there was joy. There was triumph. There was hope.

The connection reforged in the presence of the alpha, reconnecting as easily as two magnetic links. I didn't have much time to think or question. I gave myself over to the shift and let the spirit of the fox surround me.

Shifting was always a joyous, almost spiritual experience, but this time, the feeling of turning into my fox was almost orgasmic. After the fear and angst over losing my shift, being able to reconnect was nothing short of extraordinary. Relief, power, hope, and there was something else too...a burning ember that wouldn't be put out. It burned brighter, roaring to life within my heart and setting my soul aflame.

That alpha wolf was my mate.

A broken whimper erupted from the tangle of wolves and Markus skidded to the ground, his side rising and falling rapidly. A long scratch raked along his neck and blood oozed out onto the ground. He wasn't moving, and the two wolves surrounded him now, ready to finish the job.

I didn't think. Didn't have time to.

I threw myself at the wolves, knowing only that I had to draw them away from Markus.

Luckily, my blood curdling screech took their attention away from their prey just long enough for them to focus on me instead.

Unluckily, that meant I was next on the menu. Didn't really think that far ahead.

I ran, my back legs pumping and gravel flying. I had an idea, but if I didn't pull it off flawlessly...

Yeah. Didn't wanna think about that.

Markus was still crumpled on the ground, his breaths coming slower. His eyes searched for mine and I tried to call out to him as he had to me.

Stay there. I'll help you.

I moved faster and weaved in and out of the trees, using all of my agility to tire the wolves. They were only steps behind me and I could hear their growls, nearly feel the heat of their breath...

And then I made a beeline for the cliff.

No! The cry rang out in my mind.

I paid it no heed. I picked up speed even more, the wind rushing over my fur and the stones scattering beneath my paws. The wolves were gaining. I pulled my tail close to my body, praying I could avoid those terrible al

jaws for just a moment longer.

The cliff came into view and rushed up to meet me. I counted down the seconds.

Three.

Hot breath at my back.

Two.

Snarling, salivating wolves.

One.

My mate, broken and bleeding. It was all my fault.

My paws struck the crumbling cliff face and I dove to the side at the last second, tumbling end over end as the world spun around me.

There was a yelp. A crack. A cry.

I curled into a ball. Covered my eyes. The sound of cracking, crumbling dirt and rock echoed over the cliff, along with the sounds of two scrabbling, panicked pairs of paws.

A slow, tense silence stretched out for two terrible seconds. Then a final whimper. A splash. And a bone-crushing crash.

It was over.

8

FULL OF SURPRISES

S tupid omega.

Stupid, sexy, life-saving omega.

I opened my eyes, my vision still blurred from the blood trickling off my forehead.

The sounds of crumbling stone and the distant splash below brought me out of my haze and panic took hold.

Felix!

I tried to get up. My back legs cried out—yup, something definitely injured back there—but my heart raced faster regardless.

Something moved out of the corner of my eye. I nearly swiped out my injured paw on instinct, ready to fight to the death if need be.

His fluffy red snout came into view. A fox, I realized in awe. He was a fucking fox! To my surprise, he didn't run. He didn't take off for the trees and freedom.

He limped closer and lay down beside me, curling his tail close to his body and warming me with his body heat.

It didn't make any sense. Every bit of rational thought told me that the fox was nothing but trouble. That I should have let him go. That I shouldn't have cared that the ferals cornered him, and that I definitely shouldn't have thrown myself into the fray to save a prisoner's life.

But he was more than just a prisoner.

He was my mate, and denying it wouldn't change a thing.

My energy waned and I knew I couldn't stay in this form much longer. Slowly I felt the wolf side of me melting away, reverting back to my human form.

And there was my fox, also changing. He came back to himself in a fetal position, his knees clasped to his chest and his bare skin pebbled with goosebumps.

For a moment, my injuries didn't matter. My omega did.

"You stayed," I said. It was the first thing that came to mind, the first thought playing on repeat without end.

He opened his eyes and looked up at me. There was almost the hint of a smile at the corners of his lips.

What I wouldn't give to see that smile every day for the rest of my life.

"You could have escaped," I continued. "That's what you were trying to do, wasn't it?"

Felix looked away. "Yeah," he said, staring at the ground. "I mean...yeah, I wanted to get away. I didn't want to be trapped. But if you hadn't come..." he trailed off. "Your pack probably isn't going to be too happy about this, are they?"

I grimaced. Arric was right. How would a disgraced fox shifter fit in with a pack such as ours? Especially when everyone thought he was a criminal?

"Let's not worry about that," I said, propping myself up on an elbow. I didn't miss the way Felix's eyes raked down my naked body. "You're hurt."

"You're hurt worse," Felix interrupted me. "Can you make it back to pack lands?"

I huffed out an amused breath. "Well aren't you just full of surprises."

"What?" He asked, tilting his head.

"You *want* to go back to the belly of the beast? Thought that would be the last place you'd want to go right now. They know you've escaped. They don't know I came after you, but they'll be looking, and they won't go easy on you this time."

"But you're the Pack Alpha. Surely you make the rules?"

Felix turned that over for a moment. At last, he shrugged. "I want to help you."

The words swelled in my heart, but I shook my head. "Why? What's in it for you?"

He winced. "You saved my life. I'm gonna save yours."

I barked out a laugh. "So we're even."

Was that all it was?

"Can you stand?" Felix asked, changing the subject. He stood and offered me his hand.

I knew that the moment I touched him, the need to mate him would consume me once more. But I also knew that if I didn't let him help me, I could die.

The sacrifices I make, right?

I wrapped my hand around his, and his warmth flowed

into me, filling me up from the inside out. It was like I had been freezing all my life without even knowing about it. Now that he was here, I knew real warmth. I knew what it was like to feel alive.

My body screamed out in pain as he helped me to my feet and we took a few shaky steps. I tried to keep a straight face, but the pain from the cut on my thigh only heightened. Each step felt like walking on glass, and finally I had to tell him to stop.

We sat, panting, as I inspected my feet.

There was a gash there too, and now I'd gotten dirt all in it. No wonder it hurt like a bitch.

"Stay here," Felix commanded. "I'm going to get something to dress that for you."

I reached out. "What? You're a healer?"

He laughed. "No, but let's just say I've spent a lot of my life outdoors, and a lot of time looking out for myself. I can make do."

He disappeared into the brush, and even though I knew he wasn't going far, I counted the seconds until he returned.

Damn it all, I was falling. Falling fast.

"Owww!" I hissed for the fifth time as Felix pressed the healing poultice to my wounds.

"If you'd stop flinching, it would hurt a lot less."

"But...owww!"

"Guess you're not the mean growly alpha you try to be in front of the pack," Felix teased.

"Why do you care?"

"Cause I think there's more to you. You treated me like a human, which is more than I can say about my previous employer. And I just treated you like shit." His face fell, belying some hidden sadness. My heart broke for him in that instant. What had happened to him? What was his life like, that being imprisoned would be a better treatment?

"That should be it," Felix said, cinching the last makeshift bandage around my shoulder. "Now just don't do anything crazy, and those cuts should heal up in no time."

He stood and wiped his hands, regarding me. Thing was, we were both still naked. And he was still an omega.

As the tension and pain began to fade away in my limbs, I realized something else. I didn't just want to claim this man in some primal frenzy. I wanted to know him. Understand him. And maybe, the secret part inside of me hoped, show him a life above whatever horrors he'd endured.

9

CALL OF THE WILD

"I think I'll be able to walk now." Markus sat up, wincing but managing to regain his feet.

It wasn't until I'd seen him naked that I realized how many scars the alpha had. He was no stranger to fights, that was for sure. My hands lingered just a second too long as I wrapped his wounds, tracing each pale line with my eyes. They worked a criss-cross pattern across his torso and neck, still raised and shiny against his tanned skin.

Everyone said that Nox Bay was one of the most violent packs out there, but how did they know, really, if no one had ever actually seen them? I had to admit, though, seeing the fallout in person was something different. It roused a deep, aching sadness that wouldn't leave.

Despite myself, and despite the fact that he was my sworn enemy, I wanted to help him. I wanted to be there for him. To take care of him and all those countless scars.

And Goddess help me, if he didn't get some clothes on, my fox was gonna go nuts. He'd been attractive in his uniform back at the pack, but seeing him naked and vulnerable in the wild grasslands made me even harder.

It was impossible to ignore the angular cut of his jaw, the tough muscle on his arms, or the broad planes of his chest. Not to mention that (yes, I admit—I looked) he was packing some serious heat, and I don't mean firearms.

"Anyone home?" He waved a hand in front of my face and I cleared my throat, my cheeks flushing with embarrassment. Guess I hadn't been as subtle with my glances as I thought I'd been.

"Yeah?" I asked.

"I said I think I can walk. We—er, well, I at least—should be getting back to pack borders. The sun will go down soon. The ferals will be back, and in greater numbers. We can't stay here."

No. We couldn't. Those hungry, bloodshot eyes and

gaping maws still played over and over in my mind. Tonight, they'd have a starring role in my nightmares.

"I know you must think me a monster. I wouldn't blame you if you wanted to high tail it out of here, right now. I can get back to pack lands myself...But I want to give you a choice."

His voice echoed through me like warm honey, filling in all the empty cracks and spaces I didn't know were missing.

"I'm not your prisoner anymore?"

His eyes lingered on mine a second longer than necessary, and I couldn't make out what I saw there. The smallest hint of amusement, like there was some hidden joke he couldn't name.

"You paid off your debt the moment you saved my life. I'll take the heat at the pack if I have to, but you will be safe. I promise you that."

Safe. Now there was a word I hadn't heard in a long time.

I weighed the options in my mind. What life did I have left anymore? I wouldn't be able to return to the Black Hands after the failed mission, even if it meant I had to leave some friends behind. I could strike out on my own, try to make a life for myself, but if those ferals were any indication of what I'd have to deal with...

I shivered.

That left the final option: return with the hauntingly handsome alpha and join his pack. It was a risk, yeah. But I'd made a living taking risks. And if the way my soul lit up around this alpha was any indication, this could be the biggest risk of them all.

"I'll join you," I said at last, taking his warm, strong hand in mine. "Let's go."

———

The full moon hung heavy in the sky above us by the time we returned to Nox Bay. Only the night guards were awake, and Markus helped us slip easily past. I thought again about the tunnel I'd discovered. Couldn't we have used that to return to pack lands just as easily?

Unless he didn't know about it, but how couldn't he? He was the Pack Alpha...

I didn't have a chance to ask him, though, as he whisked me through the corridors and back to a large room. Even more resplendent than the one I'd stayed in, this room was lined with wall to wall carpet, a huge window overlooking the forest, and the full moon smiling down upon us.

A lush four-poster bed sat against the wall, illuminated by moonlight. To the opposite corner was an elegant armoire and a huge clawfoot tub that looked like it could have been carved from marble.

"Where are we?" I asked, though the answer was clear enough by the quickening of my pulse and the spikes of desire racing through my blood.

"These are my personal quarters, Felix. Until I can consult with my clansmen, you'll need to stay with me." He moved closer, his face now level with mine. "I can't have anything happen to you."

The sincerity in his voice was staggering. He meant it. It was...odd, feeling cared for. Back at the compound, about the best I could ever hope for was valued or needed. Only in the sense of what I could provide to the guild, not for who I was.

My lips parted, my eyes half-lidded. His delicious scent washed over us again and I remembered for the millionth time that night that we were naked. Both of us.

And that meant I didn't have to guess about his arousal. It was all over his face, but the real giveaway was the hard, jutting length of his cock.

All he would have to do would be to reach out and touch me...

"Let's get you cleaned up," he rumbled in a voice so low it made my toes curl. He stopped only inches away from my lips, his own quirking upward in a smirk. He knew exactly what he was doing to me, and he loved every second of it.

This alpha was gonna be the end of me.

Markus stepped over to the tub and worked efficiently, turning the knobs and gathering towels out of the nearby armoire.

The sight of the hot, steaming water filling the basin made my mouth water. I couldn't remember the last time I'd had a bath, much less a hot one. Resources were always scarce back at the compound. We made do with what we could. Occasionally we'd get a quick hot shower as a reward, but nothing like this.

He must have noticed me staring. Markus came up behind me and wrapped his hands around my waist in a hug. I leaned into his warmth and let out a breath. He was right. I felt...safe here. Wanted. And not just for their stupid missions. Whatever this was, it went further than a business relationship. The song I heard in his soul reached out to mine, and to deny it would destroy us both.

"Will the pack be okay with me?" I asked, still a little concerned.

"They will accept us," Markus promised. "For you are my mate." He pressed a kiss against the side of my neck. "If they don't, then we don't need them anyway, do we?"

He held me closer. The hard length of his cock pressed against my back and made it difficult to think. He wasn't the only one that was hard, either. My own cock throbbed between my legs, aching for him. Without any clothes to conceal it, my arousal was plain as day.

"Come sit with me," Markus whispered in my ear. Each hair on the back of my neck stood up as goosebumps raced down my body.

"In the bath?" I asked. The idea of the warm water covering our bodies as we curled around one another heated me from the inside out.

"I want to hold you, and my sore muscles need the heat. I'm sure yours do as well." He broke away from the embrace for only a moment, but already left a sense of absence in his wake. I didn't know how much I needed him until he wasn't touching me.

All of my skin, all of my body cried out for this man. This alpha. Was this what people were talking about when they said they'd found their mates?

Markus slipped into the water gracefully, letting out a contented sigh as the water covered his muscles. He sunk in all the way up to his neck, leaning his head back on the edge of the tub and looking at me. "Come on in," he urged me with a lazy smile. "The water's fine."

I pushed the last of my inhibitions to the side and listened to my instincts. My life and my future were here with this man and this pack, and it started here, today, in this tub.

The water stung at first, hitting my bare skin with such force I nearly jerked back.

"Ease into it, darling. I've got you."

Markus soothed me, his hands running gentle lines across my thighs and soon my back. I let out a breath and submerged myself in the water, feeling the warmth of the bath and the warmth of the alpha surround me. It was like my own little cocoon.

"There we go," he whispered when I'd situated myself against his back, his arms wrapping around my stomach. "That's nice, isn't it?"

"Yeah," I breathed, sinking back into him. I felt so protected here in my alphas arms...I might never want to leave.

Markus took a towel from the side of the tub and squirted a bit of soap on it, lathering the cloth before he tapped my shoulder. "Lean forward," he told me. "I want to wash your back."

Well, I'd certainly never had anyone do *that* before. He treated me with a gentle, almost reverent awe. Warm strokes eased the tense muscles in my back, lulling me into a state of peace.

With each long forgotten scar or scrape or crusted on dirt that he wiped away, so too did he uncover layers of me. In his presence all pretense fell away. I didn't have to pretend to be a badass thief. I didn't have to pretend to be anyone. That was the beauty of it.

Markus saw through all that. He saw *me*, and wanted me anyway. No amount of jewels or riches could make up for that.

"You okay?" He asked me softly, running small circles

on my back now with his hand instead of the towel. His touch was intoxicating—my body lit up around him and suddenly I didn't know if it was the hot water or something else that had me feeling like I was on fire.

I turned around, craning my neck to face him. "I'm good," I breathed, my gaze locking on to his parted lips. "Really good."

And before I had a chance to second guess myself, I kissed him.

Markus was hot and sweet. Just like I'd imagined. His lips curled around mine after a moment's hesitation. There was a distant splash as he dropped the rag into the water and wrapped his arms around me. I shifted in the tub, unmindful of the water splashing to the floor as I straddled him. I just knew I needed to be closer. Much, much closer.

"Mmm," Markus hummed against my lips. The vibration drove my fox crazy and echoed all the way down to my cock, now brushing against the hard planes of his abdomen. "See something you like?" He teased.

"Several things," I muttered, claiming his lips again.

He held me closer, his hand snaking down to envelop my cock. "So do I," he said with a wink.

Before I could react I was airborne, my wet, naked body clinging to his. He stood, water dripping off of both of us, stepping out of the tub with sure, careful steps.

He sat me on my feet for only a moment before tossing a fluffy towel at me. I wasn't prepared and it smacked me in the face, but it did nothing to quell the heightening desire rippling through my skin.

It was him, my mind and body screeched in unison. *He's yours!*

Well, I was about to find out.

Markus rubbed the towel over my tired skin lovingly but efficiently. When he was done, he tossed the towel aside and led me to the bed, holding both my hands in his.

"You still wanna do this, foxy?" He rumbled, a smirk playing at his face.

"Oh yeah," I breathed. I wrapped my arms around his neck and brought us both down to the bed together. "But don't call me foxy," I snapped with a wicked grin.

"Sure thing," Markus teased as he flipped me over, straddling my much smaller body on the bed now, "*foxy.*"

I growled, and this time it was no idle threat. It came from deep inside me. From my fox.

"Sounds like foxy wants to play," Markus mused as he moved down my body, worshiping every curve.

I gritted my teeth, about to throw another retort at him. Then his hand closed around my cock. I hissed and threw my head back, pawing at the sheets. Never in my most fevered wet dreams had I reacted to a man so strongly.

"What are you doing to me?" I spat, all but humping his hand.

"Oh, nothing," Markus trailed off. He worked his hand faster for a moment then let go, leaving me with that aching, empty feeling all over again. I watched him with hungry, needy eyes. "Lift up your legs," he told me, and I complied at once.

His strong arms held my legs aloft as his head dipped lower. I held my breath, focusing on the ceiling and trying to keep my thoughts straight. The moment I felt his hot breath on my hole, though, I couldn't take it any longer.

I let out a breath and it came out as a strangled moan. I tensed around him and angled my hips upward, trying not to beg. This didn't make any sense, I told myself. I wasn't even in heat!

But he's your mate. Yours. Forever.

"Please," I managed to choke out, and then his tongue found my hole.

It was like nothing I'd ever felt before. More intense than a finger. Wet and warm and probing, his tongue pressed around my ring. His saliva mixed with my natural slick and made everything that much more sensitive.

My balls tightened with every flick of his tongue, and I was already teetering on the edge when the tip of his fat cock pressed against my hole.

"Good?" Markus mumbled and looked up at me. His lips and chin were smeared with slick and the smell of my juices, and I'd never seen anything so sexy in my life.

"Great," I promised him, and wiggled my ass again for good measure.

"Felix." Markus said my name like a prayer. "Will you be mine?"

"Yes," I whispered, and it didn't even come from my brain. The word came straight from *me*, straight from my heart.

"Felix," he said again, and pressed into me.

I hissed at the stretch, wrapping both my arms and legs around him in an effort to bring him closer. He filled me all the way to the hilt and stayed there for a moment, his eyes never leaving mine. "Fuck," he breathed, and I could already feel his heart racing.

"Fuck is right," I agreed. "Now fuck me, alpha."

This time it was Markus's turn to growl. His eyes shifted from their usual color to a glowing gold as he pulled out inch by inch. "Mine," he growled, and pounded into me.

Our bodies worked up a rhythm, hips moving in perfect synchrony as we gave and took our energy and lust. Markus's cock plunged into me again and again, each thrust sending me higher still, leaving me panting and clasping at the sheets and him and crying out and —

"Fuck, Markus, I'm—fuck!" My words drowned out in a babble of pleasure as my cock erupted from the pressure, spraying ropes of hot seed between our bodies.

The sounds of my arousal sent Markus into a frenzy, his eyes glittering and a growl ripping from his throat right at the moment of his deepest thrust of all. I let out a long, low moan and sunk into the sensation. Our bodies and souls, meeting as one. Wolf and fox. Alpha and omega. His knot swelled within me and locked us together not only in body but in mind as he emptied himself within me.

Mine. My own. My alpha.

"My mate," Markus mumbled, holding me close through each wave of his orgasm. "My omega."

10

DISCOVERED

"Felix."

Someone was shaking me.

"Felix, wake up."

My eyelashes fluttered open to a room that was not my own. A bed that was not my own. Panic welled in my chest for the briefest moment and I fought the urge to shift and run, but then I saw Markus's concerned face watching me. His strong hands holding me.

And just like that, it all came back.

This was no stranger. This man was my mate, and last night we had come together so passionately, so violently, that I knew I'd never be the same again. My muscles certainly agreed as he pulled me to my feet, tossing a bundle of clothes in my direction.

So much for morning-after cuddles.

"What's wrong?" I asked, keeping my voice hushed.

"Put these on and follow me," he hissed, peering out the window then drawing the curtains closed. "And be quick about it."

I did as I was told, only because I'd been in this kind of situation far too many times before. Every early morning and late night at the compound when we had to flee or move our hideout. Every time the authorities were closing in. Every time the ringleaders thought their "investment" might be in danger.

It left a cold, bitter taste in my mouth. Somehow, I'd thought that staying here and joining Markus's pack could put an end to all that. But it looked like I wasn't done running yet.

"This way," Markus whispered, leading me out the door and down the hallway. He crept along with quick precision, checking around each corner before leading me through.

"Where are we going?" I asked him when I caught up with his long strides.

"Somewhere you'll be safe," he answered in quick, clipped tones. "I should have known this would happen."

We rounded another corner. I was trying to keep track of our steps in my head but each switch back had me feeling dizzy. Did he mean to disorient me? A clashing sound came from nearby, one I knew all too well.

The sound of a struggle. The sound of a fight.

Markus slammed me against the wall and covered me with his body, knocking the air out of my lungs. I stared up at him, dazed, trying to figure out what was going on, but he didn't say anything. His panic-stricken face said it all.

"Get down and stay there," he hissed, wrenching open a small compartment in the wall. Markus pressed his lips to me in an urgent, bruising kiss, and ran a hand through my hair. I hated that this felt so final. "I'll come back for you, but you can't let them know you're here. I won't lose you."

I was still trying to figure out what he was talking about when he shoved me into the small alcove and rushed away, out of sight.

Through a small crack in the walls I could see the

invaders pouring in through the gates, and the sight turned my blood cold.

These were not roving bandits. No. I recognized their dress all too well. Recognized the faces of the men I'd once cowered under.

The Black Hands were here.

I covered my mouth with my fist to hold back a scream. I should have known I'd never escape their reach. I should have known better than to think I'd ever have a life outside their walls. Their words crushed in on me, suffocating me in the small space.

Had they come for me when they realized I hadn't returned?

No, nothing as caring as that. They still needed the Eye, and it looked like they were prepared to do anything in order to get it—even attacking in broad daylight.

A thought stilled me then. They didn't know I was alive. For all they knew, I'd been killed in the line of duty and they'd simply sent someone else after the prize. My stomach twisted and my chest clenched. If they found me, there would be no escape. The sweet release of death would be a mercy at that point—one they would not provide.

Nothing was worse to them than a traitor.

But as I watched through the small, crumbling slat in the wall, operatives clashed with Nox Bay's strongest pack members. Some of them shifted in a mess of fur and claws and teeth. Blood splattered the courtyard.

Markus. Where was Markus?

My heart nearly stopped as I scanned the room. He fought off two men at once, his teeth bared and snarling, as blood dripped from yet another wound on his side. The attackers, however, were not prepared for the might of Nox Bay.

Fur and fangs flew, almost too quickly to follow. Then I noticed a third attacker, coming up on Markus from behind while he fought off the two Black Hands in front of him...

I didn't have time to think or reason my way out of it. Something deep inside me cried out at that moment, and I knew what I had to do. Even if it could end in my demise, I could not let any more blood be spilt on my behalf.

I launched myself out of the alcove and rushed around the corner, throwing myself at the would-be assassin.

"Stop!" I yelled, my voice cracking. "It's me!"

Everything froze in that pivotal moment. All eyes turned to me and in their faces I saw the jumbled mix of shock and confusion. Then it dawned on them. I was toast.

One of the operatives pushed Markus to the side and he skidded to the ground with a bone-crunching thud. I stood my ground, jaw set firmly in a line and arms crossed, even though every fiber of my heart cried out to go to him.

"Stop this," I said, and it's a wonder my voice didn't shake. "It's me you want, isn't it?"

Two of the men looked between each other, grins stretching their scarred faces. They muttered to themselves, but I was close enough to hear snatches of the conversation.

"Didn't know he was alive..."

"If the Master finds out..."

"We'll be rewarded..."

I gulped.

"Here's the deal," the man I knew only by the code name Shiv said. "We take you back with us, where you belong. We take the Eye and get outta here. No one else has to get hurt."

"Don't listen to them," Markus panted, still in a heap on the floor. He'd changed back to human form now, and I couldn't miss the wince of pain on his face or the lines of terror.

The remaining Nox Bay guards flanked him, forming a wall between them and me. The two groups stared one another down, snarling and waiting for the other to make a move. It couldn't go on like this, I knew that much.

It was up to me to end it. I broke through the line, standing in front of them with my hands up.

"I need your word, that you will not harm this pack any more." It was a dangerous gambit, and I trusted their word not at all, but it was what I had. And right now, I needed to buy time. If more shifters heard the commotion and came running, or if the alpha could regain his strength...

"And what do you care about these dogs? Come back home, Fox. The Master's been waiting for you, and if we're the ones to return his little investment? Let's just say that will be an even bigger prize than the Eye." Shiv's sharp canines glinted. His eyes crinkled up at the sides, far too excited about the punishment that would be in store.

I tried to forget about the bile forcing its way up through my throat, but it burned. Burned right through me, just like the flames of fear, adrenaline, and realization took me under their wings. I clenched my jaw so hard my teeth hurt. I'd found something here that I'd never had in all my years at the Black Hand Compound.

Belonging.

Even as a fox shifter in a pack of wolves, I felt safer here than I ever had with the thieves. I felt wanted, and not just for my skills or for my "value." It was still early, and a bit hazy, but perhaps in this new pack I would be more than just a possession. Perhaps I could finally have the life I'd wanted after all.

I opened my mouth to speak when a loud, rumbling roar shook the ground at my feet. I stumbled back and looked up, realizing with a sinking sensation that we'd been played. All of us.

A tall, hooded man strode out from the shadows, holding a teal-blue sphere aloft and laughing.

Shit. I should have known, should have warned them...

They'd used the attack as a distraction, and where I'd failed, they'd succeeded.

"Stand down," Shiv commanded the line of guards

flanking Markus. "Unless you want us to unleash the Eye's power, you will stand down and let us pass."

The guards bared their teeth. Clenched their fists. Even from here, their skin rippled with the need to shift.

"Face it," Shiv taunted, joining the man holding the Eye. "Resisting now would only destroy you."

Another growl. This time, it came from Markus. He was standing now, the guards only barely holding him back from jumping into the fray once more.

"You'll pay for this," Markus growled. His eyes flickered from brown to gold and back to brown again as he fought with his wolf. His pain crossed over our bond, raw and sharp. The sensations hit me so suddenly that I staggered back a few steps as well, clutching my temple.

How had he done that? I tried to meet his gaze, to promise him everything would be okay, but I heard only one voice in my mind, so loud it blocked out everything else.

"Run!"

I swerved past the operative running at me and ducked into a roll. An arm swiped out to catch me and I just missed it. I skidded across the dirt and my omega senses kicked into over drive.

My mate was hurting. My mate was in danger. But if I didn't get out of here, both of us would die.

So I reached down deep, called out to my fox, and shifted right there in the courtyard.

I didn't have the time to undergo the usual process of transformation—no time for that. My body broke and rebuilt itself in a matter of seconds without time for the pain receptors to respond. I cried out, clenched in on myself, and landed on all four feet, this time with a fox's-eye view and just enough clearance for an escape.

At least, that's what I thought. Everything happened so fast after that.

I touched down on the dirt with my paws, a pained growl came from behind me, and a terrible mechanical 'click' sound pierced the air.

"Run!" Came the voice again, and this time I didn't stop. I bounded over the fallen bodies of my comrades, keeping my eye on the escape, when the whole ground shook beneath me once more.

A savage, rushing wall of water slammed into me and knocked me off my feet. I tumbled end over end, the world spinning out of control around me. Which way was up? Which way to the surface? My limbs flailed about and caught only water and dead air. I was floating...flying...

I was dead.

As water poured into my mouth and burned my lungs, I had only one thought before blackness surrounded me. It didn't make any sense at the time, just the chattering of an oxygen starved brain, but I'll remember those words for the rest of my life:

Please let the baby be okay.

11

HOMECOMING

Cold, icy water splashed over my face and jolted me into consciousness.

I jerked upright with a ragged gasp that turned into a moan as I realized I couldn't move.

I'd failed. They'd captured me.

That was the only explanation.

The events of—god, how long had I been out?—flashed back through my mind.

Pain. Sacrifice. My alpha wailing in defeat as the Black Hands surrounded him. And on top of it all, the all encompassing, ear splitting roar of water.

They'd taken the Eye, I realized with a shock. They'd actually done it.

That could have been me. I could have been on a beach somewhere right about now, with a new life and a new name.

Instead, here I was: a captive of the only family I'd ever known.

Silk fell away from my face and the room came into focus. I squinted against the glaring lights, but I knew where I was immediately. We were back at the Compound. Didn't know how I'd lost myself in the torrent from the Eye and ended up here, but my stomach did more than a few somersaults at the idea.

And then the final thought I'd had before passing out returned.

The baby.

Shit, was I pregnant?

The thought hit me like a truck. I went over the events of the last few days. I hadn't been in heat when Markus and I had mated, I knew that much. Didn't think omegas could get pregnant at other times, but then again, he *had* knotted me...

My cock twitched at the thought. Could it really be possible? Had the alpha bred me in the midst of our passionate night together?

To be honest, the thought didn't scare me as much as I thought it would. Was it unexpected? Sure. But the thought of having a little one? Sharing my life with another and watching them grow and blossom into an adult? It had kind of a nice ring to it.

And especially if I was getting out of the criminal life, this could be my first step toward a new future. My one night with Markus had opened my eyes to what the future could be like, if I only let it.

I tried to move my hand and cup my stomach instinctively, but couldn't. My hands were bound and the restraints only dug into them further when I tried to move. I gritted my teeth and wondered if shifting would get me out of this.

No. No good. They knew better than that. An organization that preyed on orphaned shifters? They'd know how to keep us in line just fine. I couldn't shift here with the shackles on, and they knew that. Wanted to keep me docile. Keep me harmless.

Well, they had another thing coming. My shift was not the only thing I had at my disposal. I had my wits, my cunning, and if what I felt in my heart was true? The power of Nox Bay behind me.

But only if they knew where I'd gone. Only if they'd survived...

My throat closed up when I thought about the flood. Had they been able to escape, or had the waters taken them as well? Were they here, trapped alongside me in this very compound? There was no way to know, at least not from this stupid cell.

Footsteps clattered behind me and I tried to crane my neck and see who was there.

"So the rumors were true. The Crimson Fox lives after all."

I knew that voice. Would recognize it anywhere. It was the man we knew only as The Master. And that meant he knew about me. That meant that he was here to deliver my 'sentence.' I gulped and clenched my fists behind me, thinking again of the life growing inside me. Now that I'd acknowledged it, the pieces fell into place. I was pregnant. I knew it, deep in my heart and soul.

And that changed everything. I didn't just have myself to look out for anymore. The Crimson Fox was no longer a lone ranger only out for himself. I had a child inside me, and I would do anything to keep him or her safe.

"What do you want?" I spat.

"Why, I thought that much would be obvious, Felix." I froze. That was the first time I'd ever actually heard him use my name. "I want you."

I didn't want to know what that meant.

"So what?" I called out, trying to keep my voice even. "You're gonna kill me now? Torture me?"

A deadly, vicious laugh. More footsteps. He placed a hand on my shoulder and I flinched away, but couldn't go far. "Oh no, dear boy. Nothing so gruesome as that. I have a rather more enticing proposition for you." I couldn't see it, but I knew the greasy grin he wore. I knew that whatever came next would likely be worse than death.

"You're carrying a child, Felix." He stepped around to face me and bent down to look me in the eye. I tilted my head away, trying to escape his gaze, but he grabbed my chin with a rough grip and forced me to look at him.

"Or should I say...wolf fucker." He spat the last words so hard that flecks of cold spittle ended up on my cheeks. I didn't flinch away, though. Wouldn't give him that satisfaction.

"You wouldn't hurt a pregnant omega," I taunted him, hoping that I was right. They were cruel, but surely not that cruel...

I couldn't bear to think of the alternative.

"Don't you see, Felix? You've actually done our organization a great service. New blood for the Black Hands is always welcome."

The gravity of what he was suggesting sunk in. If The Master had his way, the cycle would begin anew. More children born into service, never knowing what the outside world was like.

I couldn't let anyone else go through what I'd survived. They'd have to take my child from my cold, dead hands.

"The pack will be coming for you," I snarled, fueled by the protective drive in my heart. "I'll die before I let you take anyone else."

Master huffed out a laugh, amused at my discomfort. Then he swung his arm back and let it fly, a smack echoing across my cheek and blooming into a cloud of stars and pain. I blinked up at him, tears welling up in my eyes. How had I not recognized it before? I knew life was hard, but I didn't understand just how much there was out there. And now that I'd had a taste of freedom, I saw how toxic this evil organization really was.

They were predators, plain and simple.

My skin throbbed from Master's assault and tears

flecked my cheeks, but still I clenched my teeth. Narrowed my eyes. "Capturing me is just the first step," I growled, leaning forward as far as my restraints would let me.

"In what?" Master asked in a lazy drawl.

"Your downfall."

12

THE KEYS OF LIFE

"So that's what the Eye does." Arric coughed up a mouthful of water and wheezed. "I'd heard the stories, but never seen it in action till now..."

I bit off a retort, knowing that my anger was not directed at him. He and his men did the best they could. We all did. And in the end, it was our own folly that had led to not only one, but two shocking defeats: the loss of the Eye, and the loss of my fated mate.

I swallowed. I'd planned to tell the pack about Felix as soon as possible and hope for their blessing, but I never expected everything to hit us so fast. Literally.

"Yes, Arric," I said finally, scraping a hand across my tired face. "This pack has protected the powers of water for centuries. Until now." I grimaced and crouched down, pulling away a sodden canvas to reveal a sack of grain—also soaked now, of course. I sighed and dropped it, straightening again.

"Is nothing salvageable?" Arric asked, keeping in step with me.

A snarl curled across my lips. "They knew right where to hurt us, that's for sure. Clever distraction tactics, not to mention they knew how to use the Eye...we're looking at a much greater threat than we originally thought."

"Tell me about it." Arric kicked aside a broken tree branch and kept walking. "What happened to that omega?"

I stiffened. "What omega?" Not even I could pull that off with a straight face, though. Arric saw right through me.

"You know which omega, Red. The thief. The one we captured. He one of them?"

Them. He didn't need to specify. I remembered all too well the insignia on their cloaks. The jet black tattoos on the back of their wrists.

I guess there was no getting around it. I'd have to tell the pack sooner or later, and I might as well start now, with my second in command.

"That omega," I started, choosing my words carefully. "His name is Felix. He's a fox shifter."

Arric's eyes widened. "I thought I saw a fox run off during the battle, but everything was moving so quickly..."

"And yes," I sighed. "He was part of that organization. Or is. I don't know."

We walked a few more paces in silence. That was fine with me. I still couldn't figure out what had happened. Had Felix betrayed me? Had he led them to our lair all along?

"Do you think he was a spy?" Arric asked gently.

I shook my head. "I don't think so." The thought made my wolf nervous, pacing around inside of me. "They're...not the best kind of people."

He barked out a laugh. "That's one way to put it."

My stomach clenched. If Felix was in danger, it was all my fault. I was too distracted by the damn Eye to save my mate. If I'd done something different, maybe we could have avoided all of this. Maybe he'd still be with me.

Arric stopped and gave me an appraising glance. "Red. Friend to friend. Something's bothering you."

I stared at the ground for a few seconds more, then sighed and shoved my hands in my pockets. "You always know how to read a man."

"This...Felix," Arric started. "Did something, um, happen between you two?"

"This is gonna sound crazy." My voice shook, but I couldn't deny what I felt any longer. "But I think he's my mate."

A few seconds ticked by, my heart thudding painfully in my chest as I waited for his response. When it finally came, it was quiet. Almost reverent.

"You mean like...your *fated* mate?"

"Yeah. Crazy, right?"

"Shit," he breathed. "Talk about bad timing."

I gave him a sad smile. "I know as the Pack Alpha I have certain expectations and duties. I intend to fulfill them and protect this pack and this family until the day I die. But do you think...there's a chance..." I trailed off, losing myself in the memory of his soft fur.

Arric clapped a steadying hand on my shoulder. "Fate

works in mysterious ways, my friend. And as for the rest of the pack? I'll kick anyone's ass that speaks ill of my Alpha, or his mate. You have my support."

Stress and tension bled out of my body. That was easier than I'd expected it to be. A lot easier. "That's...it?" I asked. "You're okay with it, just like that?"

"I may not know a lot about people." Arric shrugged. "But I know that fated mates business is serious stuff. So few people ever find the echoes of their heart. Who am I —who is anyone—to deny you yours? I am happy for you, my friend. Surprised, yes. But happy for you."

My heart swelled with gratitude and relief. There was still much work to be done, but we'd passed the first milestone.

"Thank you, 'Ric. But you know this makes the situation a little more complicated."

"That's an understatement." Arric rolled his eyes. "So not only do we need to retrieve the Eye and take down this organization, but we've gotta rescue an omega who also happens to be your mate?"

I grinned. "That sounds about right."

Arric cracked his knuckles. "Sounds like a party. I'll see who I can round up. What I can do. You'll need to tell the rest of the council of your plans, of course. But we're going to get both the Eye—and your mate—back."

———

We worked quickly. By the time night fell, Arric had gathered a small away team of our best trackers and scouts. I didn't know where they had taken him. There was only the faint presence of Felix in my mind's eye, just out of reach, but it would start us off in the right direction. I was hoping the trackers could pick up the trail from there.

We'd prepared guards to stand watch and assigned other pack members to continue cleaning and draining the streets. We were just about to leave when I realized we were still one man short.

"Has anyone seen Kelso?" I asked the group. They all looked to one another with blank glances and shrugged.

I furrowed my brow. He had a bit of a reputation for running late, but I'd just spoken to him not an hour before. What could he have been doing since then?

Footsteps clattered on the cobblestones behind us and I turned to see Kelso sprinting toward us, his face red with exertion. His eyes were wide and fearful, like he'd just seen a ghost, and the way he ran suggested he was running *away* from something instead of *toward* us.

"Kelso!" I commanded when he skidded to a halt. "What's this about? What's wrong?"

"I'm sorry I'm late, Alpha Markus." He dipped his head in apology. "But I just found this when I was gathering up my things to leave. Looks like its from our *friends*." His lips twisted into a grimace on the last word and he handed over a crumpled envelope.

My breath caught in my throat as I reached for the message. Hadn't they already tormented us enough?

"Is that what I think it is?" Arric asked, wary.

"If it is, it means Felix is still alive." I pressed my lips into a firm line and clenched my jaw to keep my teeth from chattering together. I opened the envelope and began to read the message within.

"Wolves of Nox Bay—it has come to our attention that we hold something you desire. You see, we have the Fist of the Mountain as well as the Eye of the Ocean now, and if you want to see the pregnant omega again, you'll meet us for negotiations. Like gentlemen."

"No way," Arric groaned. "I thought the other Keys were safely locked away with other packs."

"So did I," I mumbled, then realization hit me. "Wait a second, did they say *pregnant*?" I read the letter again, not daring to believe their words.

My omega...he couldn't be...could he?

"You okay there Red?" Arric placed a steadying hand on my shoulder. "You're looking a little pale."

"Pregnant..." I croaked, sinking into the nearest chair. I buried my face in my hands.

"Don't tell me you didn't know?"

"I..." The lump in my throat grew larger, my wolf crying out from within me. Not only had I failed him, but our child...

A child I didn't even know he had conceived.

"It's so soon," I said weakly. "How would they even know?"

"Perhaps it's a trap." Arric offered.

I rounded on him, anger flaring. My whole face grew hot, fire licking through my veins and threatening to overtake me. My eyes flickered from brown to gold when I couldn't restrain my wolf any longer.

"We're going to get him," I growled in my deepest, most alpha voice. "He's mine." I bared my teeth, making sure each man on the team could see the elongated fangs ready to rip their throats out in a heart beat. I knew, rationally, that they were my clansmen and my friends— but where matters of my mate were concerned, all reason fled out the window.

"Move out!" Arric commanded, and with all of us now together, we started our journey toward my mate...and my child.

13

OMEGA'S FREEDOM

Days passed. Or was it weeks? Who even knew at this point. My earlier bravado wore off. And with each second that ticked by, so did another shred of doubt.

Had I read them wrong after all? Was I going to be stuck here forever?

I had use of my hands now, but a lot of good it did in this crappy old cell. I'd only ever heard about the holding areas in the compound, and now I knew why no one talked about them. They were just about as inhumane as possible.

Bare stone walls. A hard, jagged edged slab that couldn't even be called a bed. A grate on the ground to catch my waste. Bland, shitty food once a day. Nothing else.

I had grown up with these people. Had called them family, once upon a time. But I didn't know anything else. Their brainwashing and propaganda had influenced me. Made me think I was doing the right thing. Or at least, the only thing I'd ever be good for.

And then, just like that...things had changed.

I placed a hand over my stomach, thinking of Markus once more.

He'd called me his Mate. Capital M. I'd felt the connection between us, promising that I wouldn't have to worry anymore. Promising safety. Belonging. Love. But if that was true, why wasn't he here? Why hadn't I heard from him?

Another wave of nausea passed and I retched. Nothing came up—nothing left in my stomach anyway. My mind, delirious from lack of food and stimulation, wandered.

Then I heard something. Maybe it was totally my imagination because I was so out of it at that point, but I chose to cling on to it as my last lifeline.

Markus's voice reached out to me from the gloom.

I'm coming, baby. Hang in there.

I looked around, but the place was still. Silent. He'd

spoken to me over our bond, somehow. Did that mean he was close?

But more than that, a fragile thread of hope wove its way through my heart and soul. He was coming. He hadn't forgotten me. He was coming.

Another shred of fear tore through me. How would he know where to find me? And even if he did, could I really put them in danger again?

I grimaced. Anything would be better than rotting away in this cell.

A metallic echo caught my attention and I looked up, searching for the source. Couldn't see anything in this gloom.

But then it came again, louder this time.

Shouts rang out mixed with what sounded like gunfire. Footsteps. Running footsteps.

My heart clenched. Could that be them? Had they found us after all?

Another rumble and a vicious crack snapped through the air. With a hiss the cell door unlatched and slid open, leaving blank, open space in front of me.

I froze for a moment, holding my breath. Was I...free? I

crept forward, looking up and down the corridor. A series of clacks and clanks raced down the hall and the other cells slid open as well.

They were here. And this was our chance.

All of my 'brothers', all the omegas and shifters they'd conned into their little organization—I could free them. We could all escape, together.

I took a deep breath and stepped through the open cell door, half expecting it to shock me or sound an alarm. Nothing happened.

I didn't wait any longer. I picked up the pace and sprinted down the hall, stopping at the next open cell I found.

"Come on!" I hissed, gesturing at the confused young man in the cell. He was even younger than I was, and from the look of him had been here even longer too. He watched me with wide, wary eyes that never stayed in one place for long.

"We're getting you out of here." I held out my hand and took a step toward him. "Come on. It's okay."

"What..." The voice came out as a shattered croak. Poor thing could barely talk. I rushed to him and slung his arm around my shoulder, helping him to his feet.

"I've got you," I promised him. "Just lean on me, come on."

We staggered down the corridor together and the further we got from the cell, the more he seemed to wake up.

"Thank you," he said at last, still watching me with those wide eyes. "But how did you..."

More shouts. Crashes. Shots.

"Hear that?"

He nodded.

"That's our way outta here."

The young man blanched, his Adam's apple bobbing. "You don't mean leaving...like really leaving?"

The idea scared him just as much as it had scared me only a short time ago.

"There's a better life out there. I promise. We don't have to stay here, and I know a place..."

He chewed his lip for a long moment. The sounds of battle grew closer. "What about the others?"

"We'll take as many as we can. Are you with me?"

He straightened his shoulders. Squeezed my hand. Nodded.

"I'm Elliot, by the way."

"Well come on, Elliot. We got a lot of work to do."

———

Mass chaos and confusion seized the compound. My heart raced with every step and I double checked around every corner, but one step at a time we gathered up our own little band of misfits.

The guards were all too occupied dealing with the intruders, and whatever breaker they'd hit during the battle had shut down the security systems compound-wide. Now was our chance to get out of here.

Our group was half a dozen strong by the time we got to the final chamber. We'd followed the sounds in the shadows, but one challenge remained: to escape the compound we'd need to go through the belly of the beast. We'd need to face the attackers head on.

"Ready?" I whispered when we came to the door. They looked up at me and nodded, then I wrenched the handle and we spilled inside.

The elders of the Black Hands locked in combat with

wolves of Nox Bay in a scene not unlike the one back at the pack. Only this time, the wolves had the element of surprise. They fought fiercely, driving the leaders of the Black Hands back against the walls, until they saw us.

Saw me.

"Felix!" Markus croaked, faltering. He paused just long enough to lose his advantage and tumbled to the ground, none other than the Master snarling on top of him.

"Protect the Keys!" Someone shouted, but I was already off and running. My fox burst out of me and I landed on four feet, bounding toward the man who'd raised me.

Master or not, *no one* messed with my mate. And as that feeling continued to surge through me, my heart pitter-pattering in time with each second that ticked by, I knew now that love was the most powerful force in the world.

More powerful than fear. More powerful than hate. And infinitely more powerful than all the mindless bullshit they'd bored into our heads. I was more than just a tool or a possession. I was The Crimson Fox, and no way was I going to lose the one person who'd opened my eyes to this new world.

I leapt right at Master's neck, my teeth sinking into the soft skin there. He yelped, his hands flinging up to grab at me. I only held on for dear life, shaking back and forth as he flailed beneath me.

"Help me!" He screeched at his men. No help came—at least not immediately. Blood oozed out of his wound and onto my tongue, filling my senses with bitter copper. I closed my eyes and clenched my jaw tighter, my claws finding purchase on his shoulders and back.

Master tore himself away from Markus and set his full attention on the fox clinging to his throat. On me. Which, in retrospect, was probably not the best idea. But in my hormone-hazed mind, all that mattered was that he was no longer hurting my mate.

"Fucking...fox!" He spat, twisting this way and that to try and grab at my small frame. "Should never have let you live, you miserable piece of..."

"I've got it, boss!" Someone called from behind us. Right before we crashed into him.

The world flew around me in a blur and we went down in a heap of screaming, sweaty bodies. The impact jarred me right to the bones, yet somehow I didn't let go of my hold on Master's neck. Blood flowed freely now, getting in my face, in my mouth, in my eyes...

A small, pale-blue orb sailed upward and out of the

man's hand, tracing an eerily graceful arc across the sky. I watched in silent horror as it fell in slow motion.

"The Eye!" Someone shrieked, and all at once three different men lunged for it.

All of them were too late.

The orb crashed to the ground and shattered in an explosion of glass and pure magical energy.

That's when all hell really broke loose.

14

OLD HABITS

This time, I wasn't swept away into a tidal wave of magical water. I braced myself, waiting for it to happen, but as the shards of glass scattered across the floor, something much more powerful brewed.

The room darkened, the ceiling over our heads turning a murky blue-black. The color of dusk, or the sky before a storm.

I released my hold on Master's neck at last, ignoring the gush of blood from his carotid artery. It splattered on the floor and he lay there, only twitching slightly, as his life force flowed out of him. Exhausted and injured, my body returned to its human state, unable to sustain the shift any longer.

Thunder rumbled above us and shook the ground. Dread pooled in my stomach. I had a bad feeling about this...

White light blinded me. Acrid burning smells reached my nose and when the spots cleared from my vision, the reality wasn't any better.

The compound was on *fire*.

Lightning flashed above us, blotting out my vision for seconds at a time. Thunder warbled through magical clouds, deafening in its rage. This was no mere rain shower. This was a storm of catastrophic proportions, and if we didn't get out of here, it would bring down the whole compound with it.

Snapping back to focus, I looked first for Markus. His hand reached out and gripped mine, anchoring me in this terrible moment.

"The omegas," I muttered, peering through the gloom. "I'm not leaving them!"

We rushed hand in hand across the room, dodging debris and fallen bodies as we went. Lightning continued to flash before our eyes and flames licked at the floor, the walls, the bodies...but still we ran.

"There!" Markus pointed, and I followed his gaze.

The group of omegas I'd rescued from the cells were huddled together in a group, backed into a corner by one of the few Black Hands left standing.

Markus and I shared a glance for a split second, and that's all it took. My mate shifted and launched himself at the attackers while I threw myself between him and the omegas.

"Come on!" I yelled, my voice hoarse. Their eyes lit up and they sprung into action, following me away from danger and toward the door.

We were so close, so close to freedom...

With an earsplitting crack, a flaming rafter fell from the ceiling and crashed in front of us, blocking the door.

I cursed and skidded to a stop, mind racing. There were other paths, other ways out of the compound, but could we get there in time?

We had to try.

A strange, tingling instinct tickled at the back of my mind, just like it had when I was searching for the Eye the first time. There was something...or someone... incredibly powerful nearby. And it was calling to me.

I reached out and tried to touch the sensation, to figure out where it was coming from. All I could feel was the thrum of power and promise. All I knew was that it was our way out of here.

"Where are we going?" Elliot asked, keeping pace with me at the front of the line.

"You'll see," I panted. Because at that moment, I didn't even know myself.

———

My dread grew the closer we got to the magical lure. I knew these halls, and that meant I knew where we were heading before the towering black door stood before us.

I gulped, staring at the one place we'd never been allowed to go. The one door that had always been locked and forbidden to all but the highest ranking members of the Black Hands. In other words, no omegas allowed.

"Are you sure about this?" Elliot asked, watching me warily. "We don't even know what's beyond that door. Might be a dead end."

I squeezed my eyes shut and tried to think. It could be a trap. It could be a dead end. But I couldn't ignore the pull in my soul any longer. Whatever was in there was drawing us in for a reason.

The door had always shone with a crackling golden gleam, ever since the day I arrived at the compound. They said it would shock anyone who tried to touch it. But today, in the midst of all the fire and storms, there was nothing. No veil of protection. Just a tall black door and whatever was on the other side.

"I don't know if we should go in there." Tristan, another of the freed omegas, stammered. He watched the door with wide, fearful eyes.

"Listen," I told them, gathering my own courage as I did so. "We are not the same downtrodden slaves we once were. We are our own men now. We are free, no longer under their control. Don't you want to see what they've been hiding from us all this time?"

That got a few rumbles of assent, but as thunder clapped closer and a crash sounded behind us, there was no more time to decide. I grabbed the cool black iron handle and pushed, leading us inside.

The door swung open easily, soundlessly, gliding across the uneven floor like silk. We poured into the hidden chamber as the storm grew closer, and only when I'd closed the door behind us did I have a chance to see what everyone else was gawking at.

The room reminded me of a temple. What little I'd seen and heard of them, anyway. It was a large, airy room with a domed ceiling and a skylight that let in the last rays of sun. Even more impressive, though, was the ornately carved pedestal in the center of the room, eerily similar to one I'd seen only a short time before...in Nox Bay...

A swirling black sphere sat on the pedestal, pulsing with life. I'd seen something like it only once before, but now I knew why it called to me so strongly.

It was another elemental artifact. One of the 'Keys of Life', Markus had called them. And it had been here, hidden in our base, all along.

My mouth hung open. Warmth, light, and energy seemed to pulse outward from it, enveloping us all in a soothing, sleepy haze.

I took a step forward, my feet almost moving of their own volition now. There were voices, faint and distant. I didn't care. I moved toward the orb, my hands itching the same as they did when I came upon a particularly juicy prize.

I had to have it. Couldn't say how or why I knew, but it was *mine*.

Another crash sounded behind us but I paid it no mind. All that mattered was the orb, drawing me in, calling me closer...

My shaking hands clasped the pulsating orb, and the world stopped spinning. It felt...I don't know how to explain it. It felt *right*. The orb glowed brighter the moment I touched it, leeching its energy into my skin, my body, my soul...

Debris rained down around us. Rocks and dirt crashed and shattered to the ground. Old bookcases, statues, lighting...

It was all falling down. So why didn't I feel anything?

I swiveled around to face the other escapees and only when I saw their awed faces did I realize what had happened.

As the world collapsed around us, we were somehow... safe. Protected. I looked up. Debris bounced off some imaginary force and scattered away. Harmless.

"What did you..." Tristan started, eyes big as saucers.

"I don't know," I mumbled, still high on the energy the orb fed into me. This was so much better than the Eye of the Ocean. So much stronger. While the Eye was just a tool, just a prize for me to steal away, this felt like an extension of myself. Like part of me.

"The door!" Elliot yelped, and the storm roared to life once more. The once impenetrable mass of black stone exploded around us. Shards flew through the air with razor-like edges, threatening certain death...only they didn't hit us. Nothing did.

Whatever force protecting us held, and I had a pretty good feeling it came down to the powerful orb in my hands.

"The Fist of the Mountain," I whispered, more to myself than anyone else. Didn't know how I knew those words, but they came to my lips as easily as breathing. Where the Eye of the Ocean controlled the powers of water and storm, the Fist of the Mountain ruled the powers of earth.

And that meant...

"Stand close to me," I warned our group, feeling the tension and power within the orb grow stronger. "I'm going to get us out of here."

They huddled in around me in a steadfast circle, defending all sides. The trance of the Fist sunk me deeper and I envisioned a way out of here, a tunnel that could lead us to safety.

And Markus too.

And all of Nox Bay.

Into the orb I poured my intention, my wishes, my love. The trials and ordeals I'd endured had prepared me for this moment. That, I now realized. I thought about the fear and loneliness of living in the compound. I thought about how I never knew any better, how I never dared to think there was a way out until I'd gotten the contract to steal the Eye.

I thought about all the young, orphaned omegas who had been used by this organization, had been robbed of their childhoods and put to work against their will.

It made me angry.

No. More than that. It made me *furious*.

That fury and indignation spilled outward, beating back the storm of the Eye and barreling outward like a wave. The walls shook. Shifted. Gave way.

And then there was sunlight. The smell of fresh grass. Freedom.

We ran for the opening, the orb's protection following us

as we went, and the moment we stepped outside of the compound onto free land, my knees buckled at the sight of the approaching party.

The wolves of Nox Bay, stained with blood and dirt, stood proud around us. In the middle of it all was Markus. He took me into his arms, holding me close, and I finally closed my eyes.

15

THE AFTERMATH

I couldn't believe my eyes.

Felix, my beloved mate, had not only found the Fist of the Mountain hidden within the Black Hands' compound, but he had retrieved it, and what's more—used it.

Yes, my little omega was full of surprises indeed.

I rushed forward as soon as I saw them emerge and took him into my arms, his body finally sagging with exhaustion. His forehead was caked with sweat, dirt, and blood, but when he looked up at me, his eyes were clear and at peace.

"Markus," he muttered, burrowing his head against my chest. "You're okay."

I brushed a hand through his hair and whispered to him. "Of course I'm okay, dear heart. I'm yours."

Felix's eyes fluttered closed, but he gave me a sated, sleepy smile. "Yours." He mumbled. "I like the sound of that."

"You were so brave, baby. So, so brave." I held him close, reveling in his warmth, his presence, his life. Felix's heart beat thudded against my skin, fast at first, and finally slowing.

For a terrible moment back there when I saw the black door collapse, I thought they would be trapped there. Entombed forever with no way out.

I thought I'd lost him.

But my Felix had risen above once more. I never should have doubted him.

"Hey Arric?" I called, looking around for my second. He was here just a second ago...

He was there, all right, but his gaze was fixed on something else. His eyes burned with an intensity I'd never seen before, his mouth hanging slightly open. Just what was he looking at?

I followed his gaze and landed on one of the omegas Felix had rescued from the Black Hands.

Oh. Oh my. A smile crept up on me and I held Felix closer still, remembering the deep, spiritual *rightness* that flooded through me the moment I set eyes on him.

Looked like we weren't going to be the only mated pair for long.

"Arric?" I called again. Gentler this time. Goddess knew he was in his own little world right now, but I needed him. At least for a little longer.

He snapped out of it and turned to me, clearing his throat and trying to hide his reddened cheeks. "Alpha Markus," he said, never losing the air of formality.

"Just Red is fine," I replied with a knowing grin. "Will you take a scout or two and check the perimeter of the compound? We need to begin making our way back to pack lands."

Arric raised an eyebrow.

I tilted my head toward Felix, now dozing in my arms. "I think we all need some rest, don't you? Why don't you take one of our new friends and check the place, make sure we haven't missed anyone." I winked. "I bet Elliot would be happy to go along with you."

Arric sputtered and turned away, but I knew his face was growing even hotter. Oh, this was going to be *fun*.

"Go on," I shooed him. "See you back at the pack."

He grumbled something I couldn't make out, but it was probably for the best. He grabbed Elliot by the arm and they left, back to the pile of rubble that had once been the Black Hands Headquarters.

———

I led the rest of our ragtag group into the woods and out of sight, keeping the pull of home in my mind. By nightfall, we'd be back within pack borders. If all went well, we'd be safe.

My thoughts drifted again to the omega in my arms. He snored peacefully, making a strange sort of snorting sound now and then. I didn't mind—it was ridiculously adorable if you asked me, but I was still worried about him.

And our child.

I thought again about the letter we'd gotten from the Black Hands. Was it true, then? Was Felix really pregnant?

One look at his calm, sleeping face was all it took. I knew it in my heart, just as well as I knew Felix would be mine forever. Our love had overcome every obstacle

144

life had thrown at us. Why couldn't we overcome this one?

As if he knew what was on my mind, Felix's eyes blinked open, gazing sleepily up at me.

"Hey."

"Hey," I repeated. "How are you feeling?"

"Hmm," he mused for a moment, then his face froze in terror. "Where is it?" He hissed.

"Shh," I soothed him, planting a kiss on his forehead. "Don't worry, we've got it. The Fist is safe with us. Didn't want you dropping it in your sleep, after all." I grinned.

"Yeah." He seemed to relax at that, and then his eyes opened with another question. This time it wasn't terror that marred his features, but sadness. Loss. Grief.

"The compound..." he croaked. "Is it...?"

"Nothing but rubble," I assured him. "They will not be able to hurt you, or anyone else, again."

"The Master," Felix breathed, wincing. "He was trying to kill you..."

I assumed he meant the particularly savage-looking man who was now bleeding out on the cold, stormy floor somewhere. *Master.* Even the word left a bitter tang in my mouth.

"He's not your master anymore," I promised him. "That was incredibly brave you know, rescuing the others from the compound."

Felix coughed. "Had to."

I huffed out an amused breath. *Of course he did.*

"Guess you're not such a hardened criminal after all." I teased him.

"Hey!" He pouted, which was just about the cutest thing I'd ever seen. "Thieves can have a heart too, you know!"

"I know," I said, kissing his forehead again. "You stole mine the moment I laid eyes on you."

Felix didn't have a witty comeback for that one. My foxy omega just sighed, rolled his eyes, and smiled.

"I love you," I whispered when it came to me, but he'd already lost himself to the peaceful bliss of sleep once more.

———

When Felix woke up again, we were nearly home. And

thank the Goddess for that, too—my arms and feet were killing me!

He caught my attention when he hissed and a hand shot to his stomach, his eyes flying open.

"What's wrong, dear heart?" I asked him, even though I was pretty sure I knew.

His wince went away just as soon as it had come and he looked up at me with hazy, love-filled eyes. "I've got one more surprise for you," he said, still cupping his belly. "But I'm not sure if you'll like it."

"Try me."

"I'm..." he started, blushing.

"Pregnant." I finished, the grin stretching ever wider across my face. "I know." The word filled me with more joy than I thought possible. Felix, growing large with our child. Felix and I, raising a beautiful little pup who'd one day become the heir to Nox Bay. Our own little family. Our own happily ever after. It swelled my heart with such hope I nearly thought it would burst.

Felix blinked. "H-how?"

"Well first of all, I'm your mate. I can tell these things, even when we're apart. And second of all," I nuzzled him closer to my chest, "it's my job to take care of you."

Felix chewed his lip. "And you're...okay with that?" He asked, tentatively.

"I'm more than okay with it," I promised him. "I've never wanted something so much in all my life. Will you let me be the best father, and mate, that I can be?"

My mate blushed a delightful shade of pink, but nodded. "Yes. I just have one more question, though. What about your pack?"

One of the Nox Bay men stepped in and talked over us. "After what we've seen here today," he said with pride, "any member of our pack would be honored to call you family. You have displayed bravery and loyalty worthy of our pack name."

"What about the others we rescued?"

"We are here for you. All of you. What you went through was vile and criminal. We can't undo that, we can't hope to. But if you and your men choose to stay with us, we can promise your our protection and support as long as you live."

"I'd like that," Felix agreed. "I'd like that a lot." He gazed at me for a moment, then said those magical words I'd whispered to him in his sleep. "I love you."

And there it was. The guarantee that I'd made the right

decision. The sealing of my fate and the future of my pack. It all started here, with my foxy little omega. "I love you too, dear heart."

Felix tried to stretch, and failed. "Now put me down! I'm getting a cramp!"

We laughed, enjoying the newfound feeling of communion and family. Who could have predicted that my sworn enemy could become my mate?

Arric was right. Fate sure had a way of surprising us.

When the kids are away, the mates will play…

Sign up here for your FREE copy of ONE KNOTTY NIGHT, a special story that's too hot for Amazon!

https://dl.bookfunnel.com/c1d8qcu6h8

Join my Facebook group Connor's Coven for live streams, giveaways, and sneak peeks. It's the most fun you can have without being arrested ;)

https://www.facebook.com/groups/connorscoven/

Vale Valley Valentines (multi-author series)

That Magical Moment

Nox Bay Pack

Stealing His Heart

Protecting His Heart

Made in the USA
Lexington, KY
10 March 2019